The Retreat

SERVING HIM

L.M. SOMERTON

SERVING HIM

Dedication

For all my readers
who like a little kink in their lives.

Chapter One

"Who'd have thought there would be so many applicants for a role where the job description includes nudity and a willingness to get your arse whipped?" Carey Hoffman leafed through the pile of paperwork in front of him. "This is a lot harder than recruiting for club servers."

"Relax, Sir. It's important we find the right people. The more applicants we get, the better chance we have of finding someone perfect." Alistair Easton, Carey's submissive, kneaded his Master's shoulders. "Our first paying client deserves the best."

"That's so good." The tension melted from Carey's shoulders as Alistair loosened knotted muscles. "Maybe we should go upstairs for an hour so that you can relieve other parts of my anatomy."

Alistair giggled. "Not a good idea if you want to invite people in for interviews this week. We have work to do."

Scowling, Carey turned to his friend and bar manager Harry Croft. "What's a Dom to do, Harry, when his sub takes charge?"

"Generally," Harry replied, "I find it's best to do what I'm told." He ruffled his sub's hair. Kai Smithson was seated on the floor between Harry's legs. "You can always spank him later, but for now, Alistair is right. We have to get through all these applications this evening. We only have one post left to fill, don't we?"

Alistair knelt at Carey's side, hands folded in his lap, his serenity in complete contrast to the noise and activity going on all around them. The Underground was always busy, but Friday nights tended to be hectic. Carey had sequestered a quiet corner for their discussion. A low table held paperwork and drinks, and cushions softened the floor for Alistair's knees and Kai's backside. Carey still found it hard to concentrate. He blamed Alistair for looking so tempting in leather trousers and a sheer silk shirt. He imagined removing the shirt, exposing Alistair's smooth skin inch by inch, then watching his lover wriggle out of the trousers…

"Carey?" Harry brought him out of his daydream.

"Sorry, I got a bit distracted. Where were we?"

"The last vacancy — if you can keep your mind on recruitment and off whatever it is you're planning to do to Alistair?" He shared a conspiratorial grin.

"Oh, yes. Right. Well, I'm thankful Mr. Wilder's requirements are not too onerous. Tor Halvorsen will act as executive chef. He cooked for Joe and Heath when they had their taster weekend with Olly and Aiden and their reviews of his cooking were first rate. Olly said, and I'm quoting here, that Tor's double chocolate brownies were better than an orgasm after two days in chastity."

Alistair and Kai both burst out laughing.

Harry rolled his eyes. "Olly would be proud. He can create chaos even when he's hundreds of miles away. That's two extra strokes for you tonight, young man." He gave Kai's hair a gentle tug. Kai sucked on his lower lip but his eyes sparkled and he rubbed his cheek against Harry's thigh.

"Tor has recruited two kitchen assistants, both, I might add, stolen from here at The Underground," Carey said. "As Mr. Wilder is traveling alone, Tor says that will be more than adequate to cover his stay and allow for days off for each of them. Tor intends to work through and take some time off in between clients. He'll also take on training Benjy and Frank. Going forward, I think we should consider rotating the junior kitchen staff through The Retreat. Then they'll all get experience of different kinds of catering."

"That's a great idea. At least they won't be shocked by anything they see at The Retreat." Harry grinned. "Right. Goran has sorted all the drink supplies, so Mr. Wilder won't starve or go thirsty." Goran was Harry's very capable deputy bar manager. "He can always take a quick trip down there if Tor needs him for anything. It's always possible that the client will want to throw a party while he's staying. Goran's already offered to run the bar for events like that."

Carey nodded. "Excellent. Then we have Luke Redding as general manager. He's ex-forces, like Tor."

"The Retreat is going to be run like a military campaign," Harry said. "Tell me about Luke. I know he's a member here but not much else."

"He's a well-respected Dom. Kept up his membership even when he was overseas on active duty."

"Well, you do give service personnel an excellent discount."

"I do, and they deserve it. Whereas Tor was in the army, Luke is ex-Navy. Served fifteen years then took an honorable discharge to care for his father who died last year. Mother passed when he was a child so his dad brought him up. He told me at the interview that he gave himself to his career, then to his father, now it's his time. He was very open. He doesn't have to work for the money but needs a purpose. He's a very experienced manager and won't take shit from anyone. He'll be perfect for mentoring the young men that will be working at The Retreat, as well as the contractors. Management of the house and garden staff as well as all the arrangements related to housekeeping and maintenance will sit with him, and if our guests want any training in a particular technique, Luke can either handle it himself or bring someone in from the club if he doesn't feel qualified. He knows the area well too — he was based at Portsmouth for many years and the New Forest was a favorite daytrip destination."

"I hope I'll get to meet him one day," Harry said. "I'm surprised I've never come across him here."

"I'm sure you will. I intend to have post-stay debriefings with The Retreat's management team here at the club."

"Good idea. So, when you Skyped with Mr. Wilder..."

"Lorcan. He prefers to be called Lorcan."

"When you Skyped with Lorcan, did he have any special requirements for other staff?"

"I think he's going to be a low maintenance client — he was reserved, but friendly. The stay is a personal reward for selling his business. From what I could make out, he's done little else but work for many years. He's had some training as a Dominant and has excellent references from a couple of clubs I know in the

U.S. He wants to see whether immersion in the lifestyle is what he wants because, as he said, he thinks it is but he's never had time to prove it to himself."

"Sounds like he has his head in the right place."

Nodding, Carey flicked through a few applications. "I've done a full background check. There was an incident in his late teens, which I won't go into here because it shouldn't cause any issues. It marks him as a survivor. He plays hard when he has the time but that isn't often. He admits to a preference for blonds. Smaller than him and not too muscled."

"How tall is he?" Harry asked.

"Six feet one."

"That rules out three of these — all within an inch of that height. There are also several brunets and one redhead in here so I'll put them aside. That still leaves six possibles."

"Whoever we choose has to be prepared to be very flexible." At Harry's feet, Kai giggled. "Not that kind of flexible, brat," Carey chided. "Lorcan wants one man to be his personal assistant, valet and submissive. He doesn't want a lot of people around the place because his break is about getting some breathing space, so this man will be at his beck and call twenty-four seven. Experience isn't needed. I think Lorcan wants someone he can mold to his requirements, so we're looking for a relative innocent — but one who knows what he's getting into."

"And who understands the difference between furniture wax and candle wax." Harry rolled his eyes. "Talk about mission impossible."

"The housework will be light, just Lorcan's bedroom and bathroom. The contracted cleaning service will handle the rest. We'll need someone bright enough to be an effective assistant…"

"And who doesn't mind taking notes naked, with a plug up his arse." Harry laughed. "Sorry, I'm being facetious."

"You may not be that far off the mark. Nudity and minimal dress are nonnegotiable."

"Well, that helps us narrow the field a bit more. Two of these applicants are house subs here. I know them both and I don't think either of them could be called sweet and innocent—they're a pair of brats. Of the remaining four, two have university degrees and one went to work straight from school but got very good grades at A level. The last one seems to have drifted from job to job but does have waiting experience."

"Drop him for now and ask the other three to come in. When we have time, I want to see all the applicants we've rejected for this job in case they'd like us to hold their details for future opportunities. It would be nice to be able to offer clients a portfolio of staff to choose from rather than having to go through this process all the time. That way we can also broach the subject when we recruit staff for The Underground. Whoever we choose this time will be permanently employed, but The Retreat is fully booked for months. We'll need to alternate between clients so that the houseboys can take some time off and that means we need to line up someone else for the next booking after Mr. Wilder. We can cover unexpected illness or, God forbid, walk-outs, with staff from the club in the meantime." Carey caught Alistair's eye. "What do you think, love?"

"The catalogue is a brilliant idea. I'd be happy to take pictures for it, but maybe you should ask some of the members what they think, too? You have an instant audience for research here."

"You're right, of course." Carey surveyed his club. The Underground was his pride and joy and he fully intended to make The Retreat just as perfect. "I'll leave the interview arrangements to you, Harry. Time for me to make sure my members are happy. I think the boss giving his sub a public spanking might go down well tonight, don't you?"

"You know it will."

At Carey's side, Alistair shivered. Carey stroked his hair. "Would you like that, sweetheart?"

"If it makes you happy, Sir." Alistair kept his eyes downcast but Carey could see he was smiling.

"Oh, it will, you can be sure of that and if you're very, *very* good you might even get to come. Emphasis on the *might*." Carey raised his glass. "A toast. Here's to finding someone for Lorcan Wilder who lives up to our exacting standards."

Harry pulled Kai onto his lap. He clinked his glass against Carey's. "Bottoms up!" He avoided spilling his drink by the narrowest margin as Kai shook with laughter.

"They soon will be." Carey chuckled while Alistair tried, unsuccessfully, to conceal a groan.

* * * *

Rowan Stanton held the cream envelope in a trembling hand. The paper was thick and expensive, his name and address handwritten on the front in dark blue ink. The cause of his nerves was the logo on the flap. Though no one else would know it from the logo, Rowan had seen it many times. The letter was from The Underground, an upmarket BDSM club in London. "Oh my God, oh my God, oh my God!" He pelted up the stairs to his attic flat—though flat was a bit of an exaggeration for the space beneath the thatch he rented from his aunt. He shut the door, dropped the latch then took a deep breath. His hopes and dreams depended on the content of the envelope and he could hardly bear to open it in case it contained nothing but disappointment. Gripping the precious letter, he scrambled onto his bed, pausing for a moment to admire the perfectly plumped pillows in their smooth cotton cases. He stretched out, taking care not to rumple the pale blue satin eiderdown, and pulled his threadbare teddy to lie next to him. "Well, Bilbo, this is it." Bilbo wasn't much of a conversationalist but he was an excellent listener. "Make or break time." Rowan slipped his finger beneath the envelope's flap, ripping it open. It contained a single sheet of folded paper and a train ticket.

"You are cordially invited to attend an interview for the post of houseboy at The Retreat. Please find a rail ticket enclosed. All other travel expenses will be refunded on production of receipts." Rowan's heart pounded as he read the words aloud. He hugged Bilbo hard before jumping off the bed and dancing him around the room. The short note gave address details, directions to the club from Westminster Underground station, a date and time. "Four days! I only have four days to wait, Bilbo!" He caught sight of his now rumpled bed cover and had to stop to smooth it. He laid Bilbo on the pillow then took a few deep breaths. It was time to get ready for work or he'd be late. He had no idea how he was going to make it through the day but it had to be done. If he didn't get the job at The Retreat, he needed to keep his boss onside. Dealing with the uber-rich clientele at Fordingby Manor Hotel might try his patience on occasion, but he loved being able to help people and the money wasn't bad.

Excitement bubbled like champagne in Rowan's veins. He took off his striped pajamas, folded them into a neat pile on his pillow then headed for the bathroom. One of the luxuries he most enjoyed in his flat was the power shower his aunt had had installed for him. The force of the spray made his skin tingle. As he washed, he sang at the top of his voice—he wasn't the most tuneful singer, but he made up for the lack of harmony with enthusiasm. His rendition of *Doing the Loco-Motion* wasn't going to win any prizes but it made him happy. He bopped around the cubicle, as much as the constricted space would allow, until his hip made bruising contact with the tiles and vibration created a cascade of shampoo and gel bottles from the shelf.

"Ow!" A half-full container landed on his toe. *At least they're not glass.* Rowan finished rinsing before backing out of the shower. He groped for a towel with one hand whilst rubbing water from his eyes with the other. He had a tendency to be accident prone but nothing was going to burst his bubble that morning. Dancing with a bit more caution got him through the drying process without further mishap. A dollop of product helped tame his hair, though it still managed to exert dominance over his efforts with a few random waves, including one rebellious lock that existed only to fall into his eyes. He discarded the towel in order to take a critical look at his reflection in the full-length mirror on the back of the bathroom door. Tilting his head to the side, he gave himself a once-over.

"Not too bad." He patted his flat stomach, wishing his abs were visible. He twisted, trying to get a view of his arse. The role specification for the post at The Retreat had been very clear. Full or partial nudity would be required. They hadn't asked for a nude photo with the application, just a head shot, so Rowan hoped they wouldn't be disappointed by his physique—or lack of it. He didn't want to miss out on his dream job because he had no money for a gym membership. Working at the hotel kept him trim because he spent most of the day running up and down stairs, fetching and carrying, but it didn't help build muscle mass. There was nothing he could do about that. Hopefully The Retreat was seeking a short, skinny houseboy with uncontrollable hair. He sighed, his buoyant mood a little deflated.

Rowan finished his morning routine, tidied the bathroom then dressed in his hotel uniform of black trousers and collarless shirt with the hotel's logo on the pocket. Black socks and polished brogues completed the ensemble. There was still time to check that his flat was immaculate before dashing downstairs to the kitchen in the main part of the house. Just like the rest of Briar Rose Cottage, the kitchen was an eclectic mix of traditional country style laced with a liberal helping of bohemian psychedelia. The units were littered with crockery—spots and stripes clashing with rose-patterned bone china. Photographs in a variety of frames fought for space with trailing potted plants, jars full of shells and sea glass and a collection of china owls. The table in the middle of the room was covered by a bright green tablecloth and stacked with piles of paperwork, a laptop and three partly full coffee mugs. Rowan's aunt, seated in front of the computer, gave him a limp wave.

"Morning, sweetie."

"Morning, Rory. You're up early." Rowan set about making a fresh pot of coffee.

"Haven't been to bed yet."

"Aurora Stanton! You'll get bags under your eyes." Rowan examined his aunt. "Too late. There's already a full luggage set in situ."

"Brat. Give me coffee."

"It's not ready yet. Give it a chance to brew."

Rowan gathered the discarded mugs, placing them in the sink to be washed later. He found two clean ones. "What are you working on?" His aunt, despite coming across as a scatty artist with a penchant for gypsy-style clothing, was a solicitor specializing in family law.

"Will dispute. Old lady left everything to an animal shelter. Daughter's challenging it, claiming her mother was senile."

"Was she?"

"Nope. Sharp as a tack."

"Well, good luck with that." Rowan tapped his foot, waiting for the coffee machine to finish hissing at him. He poured two mugs, putting one in front of Rory. "There you go. Instant revival."

"You know you're my favorite nephew, right?"

"I'm your only nephew." Rowan poured himself a bowl of Coco Pops, drowned them in milk then waited for it to turn brown. He didn't bother to sit, but ate leaning against an oak dresser that had probably stood in the same place since the 1700s.

"That's not a healthy breakfast for a growing boy. I'm obligated to tell you that as your older, wiser relative. Now pour me a bowl too. A big one."

Rowan snorted. "I think I've reached my growth limit at five feet nine. You're only eight years older than me and I dispute the 'wiser' bit." Rory was his dad's sister. A late baby, she was fifteen years younger than her brother.

"You're twenty-one—just a baby."

"A baby that has an interview." Rowan couldn't help grinning.

"For The Retreat? Wow! Go you. Come here and hug me. I'm too tired to get up."

Rowan put his bowl on the table before leaning down to receive his hug.

"You'll have to tell me all about it tonight. We'll celebrate with a Chinese takeaway. Now get me my cereal then skedaddle — you're going to be late."

Rowan glanced at the clock. "Oh, nuts!" He delivered Rory's breakfast, grabbed his coat then ran for the door. Briar Rose Cottage was at one end of the picture postcard village, Fordingby Manor was at the other. Once the home of the local squire, it boasted a carriage arch, leaded windows and extensive gardens. A review in a national newspaper had described it as 'a Cotswold beauty' — *Fordingby Manor is an ultra-chic and immensely relaxing retreat for grown-ups, with magnificent gardens, contemporary rooms, superlative food and an ultra-luxurious spa.* It lived up to the hype. Rowan jogged along a road lined with golden stone cottages, any of which could grace the lid of a chocolate box. Not that he'd ever seen a box of chocs with a picture on the lid. In fact, Rory's chocolate addiction ensured the lid of any box that made it to Briar Rose Cottage was discarded and the contents scoffed in record time. Rowan only got a look in because Rory thought strawberry creams were created by the devil in a moment of down-time between torturing the damned. He giggled at the thought, tripped on a loose paving slab then lurched into an ivy-clad garden wall, banging the same hip he'd bruised in the shower. A large gray cat eyed him with disdain from the gatepost. There was no time to stop and feel sorry for himself. He rubbed at the sore spot but kept walking — well, limping.

Five minutes later, Rowan slipped through a side gate into Fordingby Manor's walled garden. He wove a path through the rose beds, skirted a manicured lawn where Elton the peacock was showing off to his harem of uninterested hens, then rounded the fountain. He paused to toss a penny into the water, muttering a wish under his breath. His donation joined hundreds of other glittering copper discs and Rowan wondered how many of the wishes attached to them had been granted. He shrugged — he'd take a chance on anything that might help him at the interview. He shot through the staff entrance with two minutes to spare before the start of his shift. He used the precious time to hang up his coat, check the shine on his shoes and run a hand through his tousled hair. He walked toward the concierge desk in reception just as the ornate grandfather clock on the far wall struck seven.

"Good morning, Mr. Hoyte." Rowan assumed a stance with his feet a shoulder width apart, hands clasped behind his back and awaited the critical scrutiny of his boss. It was a routine he was familiar with. Alvin Hoyte was a formidable figure. Six feet four, he had fast bowled for the West Indies in his youth, regularly decimating England's best batsmen — a fact he reminded Rowan of at least once a week. Now he held court as the chief concierge at Fordingby Manor and considered it his God-given duty to turn Rowan into a first-class assistant. His philosophy for staff training consisted of ninety percent stick and a few meager slivers of carrot.

"Mr. Stanton." Alvin's deep, lyrical tones relayed his displeasure. "You are supposed to be here five minutes before your shift starts, not five seconds."

Rowan didn't bother trying to defend himself. He stood still while Alvin picked a couple of bits of hedge from his trousers.

"Have a run-in with some foliage on the way here, did you?"

"I kind of tripped. The wall I hit had stuff growing on it." Rowan examined the shiny toe caps of his shoes.

"Hmm. We can discuss standards of appearance later. In the meantime, a bouquet has arrived for the Sapphire Suite, Mrs. De Witt in the Coach House has requested tickets for The Royal Shakespeare Theatre in Stratford tonight, and there are four copies of *The Times* awaiting your attention with the iron before you deliver them."

"Yes, Mr. Hoyte." Rowan fought back a sigh and prayed that the four hours until his morning break would go by quickly.

Chapter Two

"You are the most accident-prone, clumsy, hopeless friend I ever had! Here, take this."

Rowan took possession of an ice pack handed to him by his friend and colleague Ed Sperrit. He pressed the cool gel pouch to his eye. "You're a chef. Why aren't you giving me steak?"

"Like I'd waste a good piece of sirloin on your useless mug. Now shut up and keep that ice on your face. It'll help with the swelling." Ed stood, hands on hips, five feet two inches of redheaded annoyance. "And I'm not a fully qualified chef...yet."

"Pudding boy then." Rowan flinched as Ed smacked him on the shoulder. "Hey! I'm already injured."

"Call me pudding boy again and you'll have more to worry about than a black eye and a sprained wrist. I create magnificent desserts to tantalize the taste buds of my discerning clients."

"Custard. You make custard."

"Philistine."

"Food snob."

"I can own that." Ed extracted a tubular bandage from the first aid kit. "This is the best I can do for your wrist. The breakroom is not equipped for major emergencies." He slid the stretchy fabric onto Rowan's arm. "Now tell me again how you managed to get in such a state."

"It wasn't my fault," Rowan declared.

"It never is."

"Hey!"

"So, you weren't the person who fell over a crate in the wine cellar, grazing both knees like a four year old in the playground?"

"I saved that bottle of Chambertin Grand Cru." Rowan felt he should defend himself. The wine had been worth a small fortune.

"And you weren't the person Elton chased into the shrubbery where you ripped your trousers, cut your thigh and exposed your SpongeBob underpants to Mrs. Templeton-Jones?"

"I was taking snacks to her grandchildren. How was I to know Elton had a thing for chocolate spread sandwiches? And besides, she told me it was the most fun she'd had in years."

"And this time?" Ed slumped in one of the breakroom's well-worn armchairs.

"Royston Arkwright wanted fresh ice for his malt whiskey, so I took up a bucket but he was in the bath... I was trying not to look at his bits but I had to get the ice in his glass without dropping it on him and those tongs are so fiddly. Anyway, I got two cubes in the drink but then the bubbles parted—that was a sight I will *never* forget—so I took a step back. The floor was wet and I slipped. The ice bucket went flying so there were cubes everywhere and when I tried to get up I fell down again. I caught my face on the corner of the sink..."

"And is Mr. Vickers as big as his ego suggests?" Ed fell around laughing.

"Let's just say that forestry is an appropriate industry for him. He must be right at home with all that wood." Rowan tried not to laugh because it hurt too much. "How does it look?" He took the ice pack away from his face.

"I think Alvin will have you locked in the linen closet doing stocktakes for the rest of the week," Ed replied.

Rowan groaned. "Oh God. I have an interview on Friday. What are they going to think?"

"What? You didn't tell me! For that place in the New Forest? The den of kink?"

"It's called The Retreat, Ed, and I only got the letter this morning. I didn't have a chance to tell you yet."

"Wow. You're really going to do it? I mean, I know you're into all that weird stuff, but are you sure it's what you want?"

"BDSM is not weird! It's an alternative lifestyle and, yes, I'm sure. There's nothing wrong with wanting to look after someone."

"And get your arse spanked in return?"

"Maybe." Rowan's cheeks heated. "I have to get the job first." He flexed his aching wrist and winced. "How long does it take for a sprain to heal?"

"Do I look like a nurse? I've used ten minutes of my precious break time patching you up. How about you show some gratitude and make me a coffee?"

Rowan shook his head, immediately regretting the action which sent pain shooting through his face. "I think I could have managed. But, out of the goodness of my heart, I will make coffee. Only because I want one too." He dragged himself up. "And ibuprofen. I need that as well."

The junior staff's breakroom was in the manor's cellar, the only natural light coming from a grilled window at ceiling height. Despite the gloom, it was a comfortable space with cast-off furniture from the hotel lounges, a well-equipped kitchen and a full-sized pool table. Rugs and lamps made it cozy. At eleven in the morning, Rowan and Ed had the room to themselves. The housekeeping staff were hard at work getting vacated rooms ready for new guests, while the two women on reception would be checking people out. Ed only had a short breathing space before he had to get back to lunch prep. He worked an awkward split shift with a few hours off in the afternoon while Rowan went through from seven in the morning until four in the afternoon, a pattern he worked for four weeks before switching to evenings when he worked from four till midnight. He and Ed usually managed one break together each day.

Rowan spooned fresh coffee into a cafetière. "I'll miss you if I get this job."

"Of course you'll get it. You're cute, you have this whole innocent vibe going on, and you like taking orders from men in leather." Ed grinned.

"Who said anything about leather? Though I do like the smell. Rubber too — stand me in a garage with a pile of new tires and I'm happy."

"Christ, you're weird. Most people love the smell of fresh-baked bread or melting chocolate..." Ed sniffed the air. "Or coffee. But rubber? I suppose it's good in case they squish you into one of those latex suits or a mask."

"Not all Doms have a rubber fetish." Rowan handed Ed a mug of coffee. He took a sip before moaning his appreciation.

"Oh, that's good. So what will you have to do at this interview? Is it at The Retreat?"

"It's in London at a club called The Underground. The club's owner also owns The Retreat. It's much easier to get to — they sent me an open train ticket so I can work out the best time to leave. I have to confirm I'm coming by email, but the letter didn't say anything else. I suppose they'll ask me questions just like any other job interview."

"It's not your average hotel job, though, is it? So I doubt it'll be an average interview." Ed laughed. "I'm picturing you kneeling in your underwear while some guy in a harness flogs you between questions."

"And this is why I don't take you along when I go to a club." Rowan chewed on a nail. "I never thought about it. They might want me to take my clothes off."

"Better make sure you wear your kinkiest undies." Ed snorted coffee.

"My supportive best friend. I don't have anything kinky and Friday's my only day off. I won't have time to shop." Rowan thought about the contents of his underwear drawer, inducing a state of near panic.

"You have heard of the internet?" Ed asked. "And express delivery. Do you need a brown paper bag?"

"No...no." Rowan swallowed more coffee. "I didn't think this through, did I? I mean, I understand what the job entails and mentally I'm prepared for that but there are hoops to jump through before that stage. I want it so badly. I need to think about how I'm going to handle things if I don't get it because chances are I'm going to screw up this interview. That's if they don't take one look at the state of me and ask me to leave."

"Rory will be able to lend you some makeup—you can cover up the bruising so it'll hardly notice. And they *will* want you. You have to believe in yourself. You told me once that being submissive doesn't mean you're weak. Time to listen to yourself."

Rowan smiled. "You remembered something I told you. That has to be a good omen."

"It was a one-off. Don't let it swell your head." Ed swallowed the last of his coffee. "I have to get going or chef will be finding new and sadistic ways to abuse me. I know that's your thing but I'm as vanilla as my custard."

"Jen loves you. She won't hurt you. Much." Rowan pictured the feisty head chef brandishing a ladle. She was short, plump and had the attitude of a starving Rottweiler when it came to food. Possessive didn't begin to describe her attachment to her precious kitchen. She did have a soft spot for Ed, though. She worked him like a dog but only because she wanted him to be the best chef he could be. She and Alvin got along well, commiserating with each other over the failings of their respective apprentices whilst plotting ways to make them work harder.

"I'll see you later," Rowan said. "Rory and I are having Chinese tonight if you want to come round."

Ed made his way to the door.

"I don't finish until nine-thirty tonight so I'll have to take a rain check. But give me a call if you need help shopping for underwear. I have links to some great brands."

Rowan could hear him laughing all the way down the corridor.

* * * *

That evening, Rowan sat at the kitchen table with his aunt, laptop open in front of him. "I had no idea there was so much choice when it came to clothing that hardly ever gets seen." He clicked on another link.

"I think the general idea is that it *does* get seen." Rory lifted her glass of wine in a toast. "How did Alvin react to your little accident today?"

"I think it's safe to say that my boss was not impressed by the state of his assistant. He sent me to the silver room, where we keep the hotel's banqueting plate, with a tin of polish, some rags and orders not to be seen for the rest of the day."

"Has he not learnt yet how much you enjoy cleaning stuff? Freak."

"Hey! I like the smell of polish and the way the silver glows once I'm done with it. And he does know, but he'd never admit to being that kind and thoughtful. It's against his religion." Rowan prodded his bandaged wrist. "Made this ache, though. It was a long day."

"And I suppose you've been worrying about your interview too?"

Rowan poured himself a second glass from the bottle of Merlot he and Rory had shared while they'd eaten their celebratory Chinese feast. "Ed didn't help."

"You need to ignore his teasing. That boy is a brat. Always has been, always will be."

Shrugging, Rowan brought up another page. He nibbled on his lower lip before adding a pair of wet-look latex shorts to his basket. He deleted them, then added them again. "He made me think about what I might have to do at the interview. This isn't your average job I'm going for. I don't think they'll be asking me where I see myself in ten years' time." He added plain blue boxer briefs and a black silk thong to his order then paid before he could change his mind again. He'd decide which ones to wear on the day.

"Carey Hoffman is a reputable businessman." Rory ran a hand through the wild tangle of her hair.

"You checked him out?" Rowan wasn't shocked. Rory always looked out for him.

"I did. He's a very rich man in a committed relationship with a well-known photographer. As well as The Retreat and The Underground, he owns several properties in London. He's a philanthropist as well as a businessman—mainly supporting charities related to kids. A friend of mine in the Metropolitan Police told me the club is well run and there's a zero-tolerance policy on drugs. The membership is a who's who of the gay BDSM scene. Mr. Hoffman has a lot of very influential friends."

"I've only been there once and that was on an open night. I couldn't afford the membership even if I wanted to—not and save for my own place, anyway."

"You don't live close enough to make paying a monthly fee worth it."

"They recruit for wait staff, bartenders and kitchen crew but that's not what I'm interested in. I don't want to live in London either. It's noisy and there are too many people." Rowan shuddered.

"You're just a sweet little country boy at heart, aren't you?" Rory took another swig of her wine. "Are you sure you know what you're getting yourself into?"

"I'm not totally naïve. The Retreat is about as exclusive as it gets. Even the website is secret— potential guests are sent a confidential link. I get to list anything I'm not prepared to do in the contract and there are only a few things that are nonnegotiable."

"You get the job and I want to see the contract."

"Oh, I don't know, Rory…"

"Also nonnegotiable, Rowan."

Rowan knew a stubborn, immoveable object when he saw it. He sighed. "Fine. *If* I get the job—and that's a big if—I will let you see the contract before I sign anything."

"Good. What's the point of having a lawyer as an aunt if you don't take advantage?" Rory grinned. "And I really want to see what's in it."

Rowan groaned. He loved Rory to bits, but she had absolutely no concept of privacy or personal space. There was no lock on his bathroom door and he'd lost count of the number of times she had burst in on him. Still, he had to admit she was probably right and it was a good idea to have her check over the legal paperwork if he got the job. He would just have to close his eyes and hum a tune while she was reading the details of what he might be required to do.

"I think I'm going to go to bed," Rowan said. "It's been a long day and I'm really tired."

"Soak a flannel in cold water and keep it on your eye for a while," Rory advised. "It might help." She didn't sound convinced. "Sweet dreams." Her wicked laugh gave Rowan a clue as to what kind of dreams she was imagining.

He headed up to the attic, relieved to have some time to himself. He wasn't the most sociable of people, preferring the company of a good book to a crowd. The only exception to that was the occasional night out he treated himself to at his nearest BDSM club. There he found he could tolerate the press of bodies, the heat and the noise. He loved the way the place excited his senses with the smell of men and leather, the atmospheric lighting and the tactile furnishings. It wasn't anywhere close to the luxurious standards of The Underground, but every now and again it gave him the chance to sample the lifestyle he craved. Not that he was particularly adventurous on his rare outings. He tended to observe, occasionally plucking up the courage to take part in a scene with one of the club Doms. It was why he was so attracted to the job at The Retreat. Working at a club didn't appeal to him, but the exclusive nature of The Retreat did. He could handle a party every now and again but in his mind The Retreat was an oasis of tranquility. He hoped he would get to see it.

Rowan stripped off for a quick shower. He didn't risk dancing this time—he had enough bruises already—just lathered and rinsed. He dried himself then retrieved his favorite pair of flannel pajamas from his pillow. The attic got cold at night and he was prepared to sacrifice fashion for warmth. He snuggled beneath the covers, pulling Bilbo close. He had to adjust his position to avoid making his wrist ache any more than it already did but nothing could dampen his excitement.

"How am I expected to sleep, Bilbo?" The bear gave him an enigmatic look. "There's so much stuff bouncing around in my head. If I count sheep I'll probably reach a million." He gave his pillow a good pounding until he was satisfied with its shape. "Of course, if I get this job I might have to sleep on the floor or in a cage. The client might want to chain me to the bed. But don't worry, I get my own room as part of the contract so I'll be able to take you with me." He giggled.

"I might have to hide you. I don't think the average Dom would appreciate a sub who still sleeps with his teddy." Rowan closed his eyes and imagined his ideal man. He wasn't ashamed that the whole tall, dark and handsome stereotype pushed his buttons. His fingers found their way around his cock as if they had a mind of their own. He stroked it a few times, bringing it to hardness. *If I was submitting to a Dom, he wouldn't let me come. He'd make me suffer. His pleasure would be paramount.* Rowan shivered at the idea. He took his fingers away from his erection, counted to ten then sighed. It was no good—he didn't have the willpower to resist the needs of his body. A few rough jerks and a hot gush of liquid filled his hand. The orgasm fulfilled a need but wasn't that satisfying because he had given in. He used the tissues he kept next to his bed to clean up then settled down to sleep in the hope that his dreams would be full of Dominant, masterful men.

* * * *

Three days later Rowan sat in the corner of a quiet train carriage en route to London. In his small backpack he had a change of clothes—a precaution given the likelihood of tripping over into a puddle—and some snacks. Bilbo, his good luck charm, was firmly wedged at the bottom of the bag. Rowan had treated himself to a couple of new thrillers for his Kindle and found that the psychological tension of the plot in the one he was reading relieved his anxiety about his destination. He'd had an early morning phone call from Ed giving him all kinds of useless advice then Rory had dropped him at the station, throwing in her own dose of wise words. As neither of them would be with him at the interview,

Rowan filed their comments away in a dusty corner of his mind where they shared cell space with a few of Alvin's rants and quite a few of Rowan's mother's favorite phrases, which included such gems as 'if the wind changes your face will stay like that'.

Rowan snorted. Worried that someone might have heard him, he glanced around the carriage. Only a few seats were occupied and most of his fellow passengers seemed to have earbuds in or were wired to various electronic devices. He went back to his book but found that he was reading the same page over and over again so he gave up and stared out of the window at the scenery rushing past. It wasn't much more than a green blur at the speed the train was going and it made Rowan feel a bit woozy. He wasn't the best traveler in the world—vehicles tended to make him feel a bit claustrophobic—but he didn't usually suffer from motion sickness. He closed his eyes and the unpleasant sensation faded. The rattle of the refreshment cart brought him back to alertness. A cup of coffee seemed like a good idea. The girl pushing the cart was grateful for his custom and stopped to chat while she made his drink. She slipped him a chocolate chip cookie and winked as she trundled off down the carriage. Rowan decided it had to be a sign that the day was going to go well.

The coffee was too strong but drinking it and munching his treat killed some time and Rowan was surprised when the train pulled into Euston. He scrambled onto the platform, just managing to avoid wandering into a metal pillar because he wasn't looking where he was going. He had an hour or so to find his way across London on the Tube. He'd researched the journey in advance and had decided to take the Victoria line to Victoria station then the District or Circle line to Westminster station, which was the closest one to the club. He could have walked the length of Victoria Street but didn't want to get hot and sweaty before his interview.

The press of people below ground was astonishing considering the rush hour was long past. Rowan had to stand on the Tube but enjoyed people-watching. It was only in London he got to witness the endless variety of humanity. He spoke a bit of schoolboy French but couldn't identify half the languages being spoken around him. The carriage was a microcosm of the global population, it seemed. Rowan was glad to make it back to the surface, amazed at the world beneath his feet.

He used an app on his phone to navigate the last few streets and found the entrance to The Underground without difficulty. The door was discreet and could have led to an accountancy firm or legal chambers rather than a BDSM club. When Rowan went inside he found himself in a corridor with a desk at the end, manned by a good-looking redhead who stood as Rowan approached.

"Hi, I'm Christian. Welcome to The Underground. Are you here for an interview?"

"Hi…um, yes." Rowan's nerves got the best of him and he didn't know what else to say.

"Could you confirm your name and address for me?"

Rowan did as he was asked and Christian checked against a piece of paper on his desk.

"Thanks, that all checks out. You can relax." Christian gave him a warm smile. "They aren't that scary."

"Um, who?"

"Your interview panel," Christian explained. "They want you to do well. They don't bite... Well, not much and not without permission." He grinned. "As you're here for an appointment you don't need to wear a club collar. I'll ring the bar to let them know you're on your way and someone will meet you at the lift. Actually, I'll take you myself. Let me call down and get someone to cover here for a few minutes."

He made a quick phone call, informing whoever was on the other end that Rowan had arrived, and asking for a stand-in.

"Shouldn't be long. New places can be confusing. I wouldn't want you to get lost."

A bearded man emerged from the lift then made his way to the desk. He ruffled Christian's hair.

"Ten minutes, then I have to get back to the playrooms."

"Thanks, Paul." Christian slipped from behind the desk.

"I appreciate it. I've been here once before, but I don't really remember my way around," Rowan said as Christian led the way to the lift.

"No problem. Friday is quite a popular day here, so there are a few members about. The restaurant is a big draw at lunchtime because the food is really good. Perhaps when you're done, if you don't have to get straight back, we could grab something to eat together. I'm just covering reception for another half an hour."

"That sounds great." The butterflies in Rowan's stomach had prevented him from eating breakfast or any of the snacks in his bag. He'd just eaten the cookie on the train and that now sat like a rock in the bottom of his stomach. "If you're sure you don't have anywhere better to be?"

"Not at all. My Master is working so I'm a free agent. I'll come and find you."

"I'll look forward to it. Hopefully by then my guts will have settled down a bit."

Christian squeezed his shoulder in reassurance. The lift door slid open and they walked into the noise and warmth of the club.

"Well, here we are. Just be yourself. They'll love you."

Rowan had been so absorbed by his conversation with Christian that he hadn't noticed his location within the club. They had reached the dining room and in the far corner three men sat behind two tables, which had been pushed together. They had paperwork laid out in front of them and there were four glasses of water set out. A single, lonely chair was set facing them. Rowan nibbled his bottom lip. "Here goes then." His hands were cold and clammy, his gaze darting everywhere. It was still a little early for the lunch service, but there were a few men sitting at the tables with drinks and snacks. Delicious odors emanated from the direction of the kitchen and every now and again a server would appear with a laden tray. Rowan remembered their uniform from his previous visit. The short leather kilts left little to the imagination but none of them seemed self-conscious about their attire.

Rowan realized that Christian had moved away and that he was alone. One of the men at the tables beckoned to him.

"Come on over, Rowan, there's nothing to be afraid of." He had an open, friendly smile.

Rowan forced his unwilling legs into action and took the few short paces across the room. He managed to bump into two chairs on the way but, to his relief, didn't knock them over. Reaching the interview table felt like a small victory, as did dropping his bag without spilling the contents all over the floor and revealing Bilbo's presence. He managed to smile then held out his hand to the man sitting in the center of the row. "Good morning, thank you so much for inviting me to interview. I'm really happy to be here."

"Please take a seat." The man whose hand Rowan had shaken spoke. He was tall, immaculately dressed, with dark hair highlighted by silver at the temples. He had kind eyes and laughter lines on his lightly tanned face. "Let me introduce you to the rest of the interview panel. To my right is Harry Croft, my bar manager, and to my left is Alistair Easton, my submissive. I'm Carey Hoffman, owner of The Underground and The Retreat."

Rowan nodded a greeting, relieved that he wasn't facing three Doms. Harry was also dark-haired. He was a big man and quite intimidating, despite his smile. Alistair was slender, blond and had boy-next-door good looks. There was barely an inch of space between him and Carey.

"So let me tell you how this is going to work," Carey said. "We each have a few questions for you and I'd appreciate you answering them as honestly as you can. There won't be any trick questions—we're here to find out if you would be a good fit for The Retreat, which is a very special place. I only recruit the very best staff and the standards I expect are high."

Rowan nodded. "I understand."

Carey started off with a few easy questions about Rowan's journey to break the ice. He asked how many times Rowan had been to London and if there was anywhere he particularly liked to visit. Then the questions got a bit more serious.

"Now, perhaps you could tell us why the job advertisement attracted you and why you decided to apply?"

Rowan moistened his lips. His mouth was dry and he had to fight down his nerves. He took a deep breath. "When I saw the advertisement, I got really excited because it seemed like the job had been designed just for me. I love taking care of people, and things, and my current job allows me to do that to a certain extent but… I'm a submissive. I want—no I *need* to be needed. To be cared for by someone I can care for in return. Does that make sense?" He looked at each of the men in front of him in turn. Harry nodded, Carey scribbled a few notes on the piece of paper in front of him and Alistair smiled, understanding in his eyes. "There's something missing in the job I have at the moment. There's no intimacy. I can care about the people I serve but they don't really care about me in return. I just provide a service and I want more than that. Whenever I played with a good Dom in the past, I felt like I mattered. I want to do something that matters." Rowan wondered if he had gone too far. His tone had got a little strident as he tried to get his view across.

"Thank you for your honesty," Carey said. "Now, when you read the job description was there anything that worried you about it?"

"Not really," Rowan said. "I mean, I know I'm not very experienced as a submissive but I'm willing to learn and there's not much that scares me. I get to sign a contract, and I can rule out certain things if I want to, so that makes me comfortable. Thinking about what I might be asked to do gives me tingles. Oh! I didn't mean to say that."

Alistair giggled then cast a sideways glance at Carey. Carey rolled his eyes but gave him an affectionate smile.

"Good to know. Now, I'd like you to undress down to your underwear, Rowan. Nudity, little clothing or revealing costumes might be required by our clients so it's important that we see how comfortable you are in your skin."

Rowan stripped quickly, not wishing to appear hesitant. His face was warm and he hoped he wasn't blushing too badly. He put his clothes in a neatly folded pile then stood with his hands clasped behind his back. He had decided on the plain blue boxer briefs he had bought. They weren't the sexiest garment ever, but they hugged his body and they were comfortable.

"Thank you. Now remove your underwear."

Swallowing, Rowan did as he was asked. The temptation to cover his groin was strong, but he resisted, resuming his previous position.

"Thank you. You may dress then sit down."

Rowan was aware that the restaurant was filling with people but didn't look around. He kept his focus on the men in front of him and ignored the fact that a bunch of strangers had just seen him naked. His cock perked into life. *Oh God, not now!* He scrambled into his clothes with undignified haste, praying that his condition hadn't been noticed. The twinkle in Carey's eyes told him it had.

"Can you tell me what it is that you most enjoy about looking after someone?" This time it was Harry who asked the question, just as Rowan reached the relative safety of his chair.

"I believe there's an art to service, sir." Rowan leaned forward, elbows on his knees, fingers steepled. "My pleasure comes from the knowledge that I've done a good job with grace. Sorry, that's not the right word...service should be seamless, inconspicuous and done with love. Whether it's polishing an antique piece of furniture, keeping bed linens pristine or running the perfect bubble bath, the task should be performed with the client's pleasure in mind. Kneeling in silence, assuming a display position or accepting discipline — the aim should always be perfection even if it isn't always possible to achieve. Trying my best calms me. I'm sorry... I don't think I'm being very clear." Rowan examined his fingernails.

"On the contrary," Harry said. "That was a revealing response. Look at me, Rowan."

Rowan snapped his head up to meet Harry's eyes.

"There's no need to apologize for saying what you feel."

"May I, Sir?" Alistair turned to Carey.

"Of course, love."

Rowan immediately felt more at ease. Alistair was a sub so he would understand how Rowan felt.

"Rowan, The Retreat is quite isolated and very rural. How do you think you'll cope with that?" Alistair's tone was gentle and reassuring.

"I'm a country boy. I live in a small village and work at a country hotel. Cities scare me. There are too many people and the noise never stops. Oh... I guess you guys like that, though."

Alastair giggled. "It has its moments." He frowned. "In this role, you would only get time off between clients because we want continuity of service for each guest. Sometimes that might mean working for a few days or a week but other times for a month or more. How do you feel about that?"

"I like the idea that I can get to know a client during his stay. The better I know someone, the better the service I can provide. And, to be honest, I tend to get a bit territorial. I know other people are just as capable as me but I have a hard time accepting that they care as much. If I had time off I would feel like I was abandoning my client."

Alistair nodded. "Thanks, Rowan."

After a few more probing questions from Harry, Carey asked, "Do you have any final questions for us?"

"Just…well…would I get any information about the clients before their arrival? So I could prepare things to their liking?"

"We have very strict confidentiality agreements," Carey said, "which you would have to sign. The client's identity is only revealed at their discretion and they may choose to use a false name. You would receive a folder containing details of their preferences. When a client books a stay at The Retreat, they get to select any number of things to make their stay more enjoyable. This could also affect your working conditions so we would share that with you."

Rowan nodded. "Thank you. It all sounds wonderful."

Carey stood, offering a hand. "That's it for now. I can see Christian waiting for you."

"We're having lunch together."

"That's a great idea — you can ask him anything else you think of. Please accept the meal with our compliments. We'll be in touch very soon."

Rowan shook Carey's hand before grabbing his bag. "Yes, sir. Thank you for the opportunity." He nodded to Harry and Alistair before moving away, searching the room for Christian. He was standing to one side near the kitchen door and gave Rowan a small wave. Rowan walked across to him, taking care not to knock into anything.

"How did it go?" Christian asked.

"I've no idea," Rowan replied. "I mean, I answered all their questions but I'm not sure I was giving them the answers they were looking for. I was too nervous to make eye contact very much so it was hard to tell how they were reacting."

"Well, I'm sure you did really well and you deserve a nice lunch, so let's find a table then you can choose whatever you like from the menu." Christian led him across the restaurant to a table set for three. "I hope you don't mind but I asked another friend to join us. His name's Olly and I'm sure you'll like him—everyone does. He's here with his Dom, Joe, but he has permission to spend some time with us."

"Sure," Rowan replied. "I don't get to meet many subs and it's really nice to be with people who understand me."

"He should be here in a few minutes."

Christian took a seat and Rowan chose the one next to him, facing out into the restaurant so he could indulge in a bit of people-watching.

"Here, have a look at the menu." Christian handed it over. "The chefs are brilliant. I don't think there's anything I wouldn't recommend. Except avocado—I hate those things."

Rowan chuckled at Christian's grimace. He examined the extensive list of dishes. "Wow, there's so much choice! A lot more than in the restaurant at the hotel where I work."

"It's a bit overwhelming, isn't it? Carey usually orders for me because I can never make up my mind. If you like, we could get one of the sharing platters. Lots of yummy, deep-fried finger food with a selection of dips. You can choose between meat, fish or vegetarian. Do you have a preference?"

"Fish! Because the garlic prawns are incredibly scrummy."

Rowan glanced up from the menu to see who had spoken because it wasn't Christian. Someone, who he guessed must be Olly, had joined them and was pulling up a chair. The young man had a head of golden curls, blue eyes and a cheeky grin. He wore tight black leather trousers, glittery lilac Vans and a purple T-shirt with a rainbow-colored unicorn on it.

"Hi, I'm Olly, and I'm serious—the fish platter is scrumplicious."

"Rowan." Rowan couldn't help but smile. Olly seemed so full of joy it was bubbling over.

"Christian told me that you're going to need lots of sympathy because you've just been through a horrible ordeal. I'm really good at sympathy because I'm a nurse so I've been trained in how to be nice to people." Olly cocked his head to one side as if thinking hard. "Though some of the soldiers at the military hospital where I work every now and again say that my bedside manner could be improved, but it's hardly my fault when they can't aim vomit into a paper bowl. You'd think being soldiers they'd be good shots but no. I dread to think what they're like in the gents." He giggled. "Anyway, I will definitely be nice to *you*. I can't imagine what it must be like to be interviewed by Harry and Carey. The idea terrifies me. Though, if Alistair was there it couldn't have been all bad because he's really sweet—that's if the dommy types let him get a word in edgeways. My Dom is Joe. He's over there at that table."

Olly leaned so far back in his chair that Rowan held his breath, thinking that it would tip over any second. Olly pointed at a handsome blond man on the other side of the room, sharing a table with three others.

"Isn't he gorgeous?" He rocked his chair back into place. "I'm a very lucky boy. But I have to be good and eat healthy things, so if we're having one of the sharing platters, and I really, really hope we are, then we have to get salad too. That counts as healthy, doesn't it? And fish is good for me, it has all that omega three stuff. And if I eat all that good stuff it means I can have a really big dessert." He rubbed his flat stomach with both hands, eyes bright with excitement. "So tell us all about the interview. What mean questions did they ask you? Was it like an interrogation, you know like the Spanish Inquisition with torture and stuff?" He shivered. "That would be so delicious."

Rowan laughed. "There was no torture involved, though I did have to take my clothes off in front of the whole restaurant."

Olly gasped. "Holy guacamole! Joe would never let me do that. He says that my special bits are for his eyes only. Of course, his eyes get to see them a lot. When we are at home he has this strange idea that clothing is optional for me, but not for him, which I don't think is fair because he has the most amazing body, which I really, really like to look at, and kiss, and lick..." Olly got a dreamy look on his face as if he was off in another world.

"Too much information, Olly," Christian said, grinning.

"But we're friends," Olly said, "and friends tell each other everything. I keep saying that to Aidan, he's my best friend, Rowan, but he's not here because he's back in Yorkshire working. He has a brain the size of Jupiter and does really clever computer geeky stuff, which I don't understand, and he lives in the basement but I think he likes it down there because it reminds him of the dungeon and he spends a *lot* of time in dungeons with his Dom, Heath."

Christian shook his head. He waved to the nearest server who scurried over. "Can we get the fish platter for three please, Barnaby? And a big bowl of mixed salad with some of the chef's special dressing. Water okay for everyone, or would you prefer juice?"

"Water for me, please," said Rowan.

"I'll take an apple juice with ice," Olly said.

Barnaby smiled then skipped toward the kitchen. His kilt lifted as he moved, revealing his almost bare arse. Several diners at other tables turned to watch him.

"I don't think it'll be long before Barnaby finds himself a Master," Christian commented. "Several members have shown interest already."

"Do many people get paired up after working here?" Rowan asked.

"Quite a few," Christian responded. "That's why they are constantly having to recruit. I used to work reception here before I met my partner and now I just cover when they're a bit short-staffed. I'm at college most of the time."

"But it will be different at The Retreat," Olly said. "I can't imagine anyone wanting to work somewhere else after they've spent time there—it's an amazing place."

"Have you been?" Rowan was intrigued.

"I have," Olly said. "Not that long ago either. Me and Joe, Aidan and Heath went to stay there for a long weekend. Carey wanted a few friends to test out some of the facilities before he opened to paying guests. It wasn't fully staffed, but the chef was there and he can work magic in the kitchen. I can't tell you how orgasmic his double chocolate brownies are." Olly smacked his lips together. "The bedrooms are amazing, too. They all have their little secrets and look like normal guest bedrooms if you don't examine them too closely."

"What do you mean?" Rowan asked.

"Well, in one room there's a priest's hole in the floor, which has been converted to a cage. Aidan spent some time in there." Olly grinned. "And in the room Joe and I shared there was a sling hidden in the canopy of the four-poster and a piece of furniture that converted to a spanking bench. Just perfect. We had an amazing time. Oh, and you must visit the attic. But I won't give away all the place's secrets—some of them you need to discover for yourself."

"I haven't got the job yet," Rowan said. "But I'm keeping everything crossed."

"That must be really uncomfortable," Olly said, crossing his eyes.

Their food arrived and the three of them tucked in. Rowan found that he had a voracious appetite. As Christian had promised, the food was delicious and there was plenty for all of them. They chatted about all kinds of things during the meal and Rowan felt like he'd made two good friends even in such a short space of time. Christian was serene and calm, he made Rowan feel relaxed and Olly was so much fun, Rowan couldn't imagine anyone not liking him—though he thought it would probably be quite easy to get into trouble if he spent much time with him. They were perusing the dessert menu when Alistair came over.

"Mind if I join you?" he asked.

"Alistair!" Olly jumped to his feet and gave Alistair a hug. "Of course you can, even though you were part of the Inquisition." His eyes sparkled.

"Thanks, I think." Alistair gave a wry grin. "I'll have the strawberry tart if you're ordering desserts but I've also come with good news. Congratulations, Rowan, the job at The Retreat is yours if you want it."

Rowan gaped. "But I wasn't expecting to hear anything for days."

"You were the last person we had to interview, and it was a really easy decision. We all agreed you'd be perfect for the post."

Rowan didn't know what to say. He was shocked, happy and nervous all at once. Christian and Olly both congratulated him, Christian with a hug and Olly with a big kiss on the cheek. "I... Um..."

"Time for pudding." Olly waved at Barnaby. "We need three giant chocolate surprises and one boring piece of strawberry tart," he said. "We're celebrating."

While Barnaby went to the kitchen to sort out their order, Alistair grabbed a chair from a vacant table and they all shuffled around to make room for him.

"You're going to get into so much trouble for this, Olly." Alistair winked. "I hope you haven't been taking on board any advice that Olly is giving you, Rowan, he's a bad influence."

"I am." Olly raised his glass of juice in a toast. "And proud of it. But I'm sure Rowan wouldn't be swayed by little old me."

Rowan laughed. "I think, Olly, that you might look angelic but you're the devil in disguise."

Christian and Alistair fell about laughing.

"He's got you down to a T," Christian said.

Olly tossed his head, making his blond curls bounce. "I'm sure I don't know what you mean. I'm as pure and innocent as the driven snow."

Their desserts arrived and Rowan gaped at their size. Conical sundae dishes contained layers of chocolate mousse, cherries, cream and chunks of brownie, and were topped with a smooth dark ganache and more cherries. "There's no way I'm going to be able to fit this in," Rowan said.

"Well, if you run out of room, I'd be happy to help you out," Olly said.

"Olly's never met a dessert yet that could beat him," Christian commented.

"Puddings are made to be conquered," Olly announced. "Whether they are in pretty glass dishes or smeared on Joe's abs." His expression was deadly serious.

Trying not to laugh, Rowan scooped a spoonful of the sweet concoction into his mouth and before he knew it, he was scraping the bottom of the dish.

"You see? Rowan and I are destined to be soulmates." Olly gave his spoon a final lick. "We should get coffee now."

"You might want to rethink that," Christian said, "because Joe and Carey are heading this way."

"Oh." Olly's eyes widened. He sipped some water. "Do I have any chocolate around my mouth?" He licked his lips.

Rowan resisted the urge to stand up as Carey and Joe approached. Close-up, Rowan could now see that Olly's Dom was startlingly good-looking, with icy pale blue eyes. He could have come across as haughty and cold but when his gaze rested on Olly the chill in his eyes warmed.

"I hope you all had a lovely lunch," Carey said. "Were you impressed by the cooking, Rowan?"

"Yes, sir. Everything was delicious. I think it was one of the best meals I've ever eaten."

"The chef will be delighted to hear it," Carey said. "And congratulations on your new role, not that I would assume to pre-empt your decision. However, I've taken the liberty of putting together some paperwork for you." He handed over a folder. "In there you'll find a contract of employment with a covering letter and a separate contract with the more unusual details of the role. Please take your time and have someone else look over them if you wish. I'd appreciate a quick phone call, once you've made your decision, to let me know whether or not you'd like to accept the job."

"Of course, sir. If my aunt—she's a lawyer—is happy with the paperwork, I'll definitely be accepting. I can't tell you how delighted I am that you've offered the role to me."

"We interviewed several candidates but you stood out, Rowan. I'll be very pleased to have you as part of the staff at The Retreat. I think you'll fit in extremely well." Carey smiled. "Can I introduce you to Joe Dexter? The reprobate sat next to you is his sub."

"It's very nice to meet you, sir. Olly is great company. Thank you for allowing him to have lunch with me. He ate lots of salad."

Joe shook his head. "That's another one you've corrupted then, Oliver. I know exactly what you've been eating. Barnaby is an excellent spy. So it's fortunate that I've managed to secure one of the private rooms for the afternoon because your punishment is going to take a while."

Rowan felt a moment's anxiety that his new friend was in trouble but relaxed when he caught sight of the grin Olly was trying to hide.

"I think that's my signal to leave," Olly said. "It was delightful to meet you, Rowan, and a wonderful coincidence that I happened to be here in London at the same time as you. It must have been fate, don't you think?" Olly rose gracefully from his chair and turned into Joe's arms, melting against him and resting his head on Joe's shoulder. Rowan didn't think he'd ever seen a couple so obviously in love. He watched them walk away, feeling just a little jealous.

"Joe and Olly are engaged to be married," Christian explained. "Their engagement party was spectacular. I can only imagine how fabulous the wedding will be."

"I like him," Rowan said. "I think he must be a very special friend." He checked his watch. "I really need to go and catch a train if I'm going to get home at a decent hour. I have to work in the morning and I have a really early start." He stood up. "Thank you for making me feel so at home. I hope I'll get to see you both again." He checked his bag, making sure Bilbo was still safely tucked away. He slipped the folder in beside his spare clothes. "I'll read everything on the train on the way home." Christian and Alistair both wished him a safe journey and within a few minutes he was back outside in the London streets, surprised to find that it was still daylight. He felt like he was walking on air and couldn't wait to get home to relay his news to Rory and Ed. He patted his rucksack. "Bilbo the good luck charm strikes again!"

Chapter Three

Rowan stood outside Briar Rose Cottage, two bulging holdalls at his feet. He couldn't believe how time had flown since his interview at The Underground. It had been almost a month but felt more like five minutes since he'd returned from London and handed in his notice to Alvin at the hotel. Rowan had been flattered when Alvin had tried to persuade him to change his mind and stay but even the prospect of new responsibilities and a raise couldn't tempt him. He hadn't given Alvin all the details about his new role, just that it would give him an opportunity to provide more personal service to guests at a smaller, more intimate establishment. Alvin hadn't pressed for more information and at Rowan's leaving party, organized by Ed, he'd given a touching speech about how he hoped his training might influence Rowan's career in the future.

Ed had been almost as excited as Rowan when he'd heard the news about his success. On his night off he'd come round to the cottage. He and Rowan had camped out on Rowan's bed with pizza, ice cream and fizzy drinks in a variety of chemically enhanced colors. Ed had insisted that Rowan give him a second by second commentary of his entire visit to London. He'd wanted to know every detail.

"If I didn't know better," Rowan said, "I'd think you were hankering after a job at The Retreat too. You seem awfully interested in what I'm going to be doing."

Ed waved a floppy piece of pizza at him. "Let's just say I want to live vicariously through you. I'm basically a galley slave, so I think my career path has some similarities to yours." He chuckled.

"I'm not going into slavery," Rowan protested. "Though…that can be an element of the lifestyle." Teasing Ed was fun. "Seriously, I'm not losing my freedom here. It's a job — just a little different from the norm. Besides, I swear Rory went over the contracts with a magnifying glass. She checked every letter. Twice." He grabbed another slice of ham and mushroom before Ed could steal it. "From a legal perspective, she said the contracts were more than fair. In fact if she'd been working for Mr. Hoffman, she would have advised him to make them slightly less favorable."

"I'm just jealous." Ed flopped onto his back.

"If you keep eating pizza like that, you're going to choke and then I'll be minus one best friend. Sit up, for goodness sake."

"Yes, Mother." Ed shoved some pillows behind his back and got a bit more upright. "I'm going to miss you, and yes I know I sound whiny."

"I'll miss you too," Rowan admitted. "But I'll have my phone with me. We can talk every night if you want to."

"Might be difficult if your client has a fondness for ball gags." Ed managed to keep a straight face for all of ten

seconds before he dissolved into hysterical laughter. Rowan sighed. He grabbed Bilbo for a hug.

"I get more sense out of you, Bilbo."

Since that night, Ed had teased Rowan continuously. Rowan suspected he had been cruising the leather shops online because he seemed to have gained rather an extensive knowledge of BDSM equipment and toys. Just thinking about some of their discussions in the staff breakroom made Rowan laugh. He thought his vanilla-flavored friend might just be discovering his kinky side.

Rowan had discovered his love of kink much, much earlier. He'd been eighteen, brand-new to the gay dating scene, and had stumbled across the only leather bar in the nearest town. He could still recall that evening, the new sights, sounds and smells which had tantalized his senses and fired his imagination. He'd been scared out of his wits at the uninhibited approaches from men twice his age, then an older guy in beaten-up leathers who went by the name of Axel had bought him an orange juice before giving him a running commentary on the action. Axel had become a good friend, as had his long-term partner and submissive, Franz. Without them, Rowan was under no illusion that he would have been eaten alive. His introduction to the scene had been gradual, gentle and educational. He'd avoided those sites on the Internet that purported to reflect the lifestyle but were actually fantasy and learned from men who lived BDSM twenty-four seven. He'd been fortunate and he knew it. He'd always be grateful to the people who'd shared their lives and experiences with him, teaching him to be comfortable in his own skin.

"And now here I am." Rowan stared down the road. Once all his paperwork had been completed, Carey had called him to let him know that a car would be sent to collect him, to take him to Hampshire. Rowan had been expecting a taxi, but the car that pulled up at the curb next to him was a sleek, black limousine with tinted windows. Rowan gaped—he couldn't believe the car was for him—but then the driver's door opened and a chauffeur, dressed in a smart gray uniform complete with peaked cap, got out.

"Mr. Stanton?"

Rowan nodded. "Yes, that's me."

"You're expecting a ride to The Retreat?" The chauffeur gave him a cheeky grin, then winked. "Not one of the Doms on the staff then? I'm Rayne, that's r-a-y-n-e," he spelled. "Not rain the weather. Suppose I should be grateful for that. It's a small mercy because my parents were a pair of pot-smoking hippies and I could have ended up being Rainbow Moonchild or something. In fact, they're still a pair of hippies, they aren't dead or anything."

Rowan chuckled and took a closer look at his driver. A mop of light brown hair stuck out from beneath Rayne's cap. He had brown eyes, a scattering of freckles across the bridge of his nose and lips that seem to be curved permanently into a smile. He was about Rowan's height, but a little broader in the shoulders.

"Nice to meet you." Rowan spoke before Rayne wondered about the amount of staring going on.

"Those your bags?" Rayne gestured to Rowan's holdalls. He didn't wait for an answer but popped the boot then placed both bags inside. "You travel light."

"I'm the houseboy," Rowan said, hoping that was adequate explanation.

"Ah, so you won't be needing that much in the way of clothes then, except for days off and in between clients of course." Rayne held the back door of the car open. "In you get."

"Oh… Can't I travel in the front with you?"

Rayne grinned. "Of course you can. Your wish is my command, at least for the length of this journey anyway."

Rowan relaxed into the plush leather seat — it was the most luxurious car he'd ever been inside. "This must be great to drive."

"It is. When I got the job I couldn't believe this would be mine to look after. I'm a bit of a petrol head, so it's a dream come true."

"So what will you be doing at The Retreat?" Rowan asked.

"Personal chauffeur for the clients," Rayne replied. "While they are in residence, I'm on call twenty-four hours a day to take them wherever they want to go. When I'm not needed by the clients I'll run errands for the manager."

"And do you have…any other duties?" Rowan wasn't brave enough to ask the question he really wanted to.

"You mean any of the kinky stuff?" Rayne laughed. "I think that's more your line, but let's just say if any of them have chauffeur fantasies I'll be quite happy to oblige. I just hope that if they want me to wash the car in my birthday suit, they wait for a warm day." He rolled his eyes.

"How did you find out about the opening?"

"I was working for the private hire firm that Carey uses for members of The Underground when they need a car. One day I had to go into the club to find a client and that was that. I liked what I saw and joined the next day. Carey gave me an amazing deal on membership. Then when the driving job for The Retreat came up, he asked me if I'd be interested. I don't even mind the uniform."

The journey to Hampshire went by like a flash. Rayne was great company and chatted most of the way. He was much more outgoing than Rowan, but he listened too and asked Rowan lots of questions about why he'd chosen to take the job at The Retreat. He also told Rowan as much as he could about the other staff who were already in place. Rowan was a little nervous about meeting Tor, the chef, and the man he would be reporting to, Luke Redding, but Rayne insisted that they were both approachable and patient.

Rowan's parents had taken him on holiday to the New Forest when he was about ten, but he hadn't been back since. He loved the dappled light cast by the trees over the lanes and even caught a glimpse of some ponies. It was a beautiful part of the country. Entry to The Retreat was gained through huge wrought-iron gates with the name of the place worked into the metal. They swung open as the car approached. "Number plate recognition," Rayne explained at Rowan's curious glance. "Security here isn't obvious, but the guests' privacy is guaranteed. There are quite a few cameras around the place and some silent alarms."

Rowan looked eagerly for his first view of the house, though it was a while before the building came into view. Rayne had described it but it more than exceeded Rowan's expectations. The Gothic mansion sat at the center of a vast clearing in the forest. The ivy-clad golden stone glowed in the sunlight. Towers, turrets and arches sprouted from a mismatched set of buildings, giving Rowan the impression of a fairy-tale castle.

"It's spectacular!"

"It is impressive, isn't it?" Rayne guided the car beneath an elaborate stone portico into a wide courtyard, parking in front of an open porch. Rowan could just see the arched, wooden front door, furnished with black iron hinges and handle. "I'll put your luggage in the porch. I'm sure Mr. Redding will be out to meet you shortly. I have to go clean the car then put it away because it's not needed for the rest of the day. I have to be up early to get to the airport to collect our client."

"Thanks for bringing me," Rowan said. "I really enjoyed the journey."

"I get the feeling we're going to be great friends. I don't know what Luke's plan is for you today, but I'll be in for supper later so I might see you then." Rayne got out of the car, unloaded Rowan's bags from the boot then waved as he drove off, leaving Rowan standing next to them. Rowan examined what he could see of this new home, delighting in all the historic architectural details. The building was quirky but beautiful and he couldn't wait to see inside.

He spun around as the door behind him opened. Only the slightest creak of the hinges had given the movement away. The man standing in the doorway was tall, Rowan guessed at least six-three. He had a military bearing, holding himself very straight with his shoulders pushed back. His handsome features caught Rowan's attention, but it was his eyes that captured Rowan's gaze. They were a clear shade of green that Rowan hadn't often seen and seemed to drill through to his soul. It was all Rowan could do to maintain eye contact and not look away.

"Good morning. You must be Rowan Stanton. I hope you had a pleasant journey."

"Yes, thank you, sir. Rayne was very kind and the trip passed quickly."

"Rayne is a chatterbox, but a great chauffeur. As you've probably worked out, I'm Luke Redding, the general manager. I'll be taking you through your induction today."

Rowan gulped. This man was his new boss and he was a little scary. Other than his name, Rowan didn't know anything about him. Carey Hoffman had mentioned him in the letter about Rowan's travel arrangements, but that was all. Rowan's instincts told him Luke was a Dom. He exuded a sense of complete control and didn't seem like anything, short of a major natural disaster would faze him. In fact, Rowan could imagine him as the hero in any number of bad end-of-the-world movies he and Ed had watched on the Syfy Channel.

"Would you like to come in, or would you prefer to stand there staring for the rest of the day?" Luke asked.

"Oh! Sorry… It's just that there's so much to take in." Rowan grabbed his bags then heaved them into the entrance hall, following Luke's lead. In front of him a double staircase swept upward in graceful curves to a galleried landing. A spectacular, circular stained-glass window was set in the wall above the gallery, casting multicolored streams of light across the hall.

"There are five guest bedrooms, all accessed via the gallery," Luke explained. "But I'll take you through to the staff quarters first. You can leave your bags in your room and there will be time later this evening for you to unpack. As our guest arrives tomorrow, I'll give you a full tour then some time to explore on your own because it's important that you know the building well. Of all the staff here, you will have the most direct contact with Mr. Wilder and if he asks you a question you need to be able to answer it. After lunch, we'll spend some time together and I will give you a briefing on Mr. Wilder's likes and dislikes and on the duties you will be required to carry out around the house. Do you have any questions?"

Rowan had hundreds, but none that he felt able to ask at that moment. It was the first time he'd heard the client's name, which sounded dangerous and exciting. He shook his head. "No, not right now, thank you, sir."

Luke led him through a labyrinth of corridors, then up a flight of stairs to a plush, carpeted passage giving access to several doors.

"Your room is at the far end." Luke pushed the door open then held it so that Rowan could get inside with his bags, which he immediately placed on the floor. The room was much larger than he had expected, square in shape with a double bed, fitted wardrobe and large chest of drawers. It was decorated in calming shades of cream and green and the bed was covered by a bright quilt and a stack of pillows. "This is your space," Luke said. "No one will come in here without your permission. There's no lock, but you have no need to worry about security. Depending on Mr. Wilder's requirements, it could be that you spend very little time in here. His needs must come first but if he doesn't require your services, and you have completed your duties, you are free to come here as you wish."

Rowan wandered over to the window where there was a beautiful view of the forest. The Retreat was isolated, no doubt about it, but Rowan found that comforting. The window was open a fraction and for a moment, Rowan listened to the sounds filtering in from outside that were so different from home. He imagined that the constant rustle of the leaves must be like living close to the sea, where continuous, familiar noise lingered at the back of your mind whilst not being intrusive. "I think I'm going to like it here." He spoke only to himself, but Luke heard him.

"I hope so. Not everyone deals well with the tranquility, but life moves at a slower pace here. You'll be busy, but there's none of the frantic pressure of the city."

Rowan explored his room a little more, discovering an en suite bathroom with a full-size tub and separate walk-in shower. He hadn't expected nearly so much luxury for his own accommodation and, as if sensing his surprise, Luke gave a low chuckle.

"Mr. Hoffman treats his staff extremely well. In return, he and I expect you to work hard and give the service our guests expect." He turned toward the door. "Come with me. We've a lot to get through today."

Rowan followed obediently. Luke had a way of speaking that demanded compliance without being aggressive and Rowan's submissive nature responded to the tone, which made him feel safe somehow. He had to move quickly to keep up with Luke, who set a rapid pace.

"We'll start in my office, which is where I will give you a briefing before every new client. I'll also expect you to report to me at least once a week. We'll arrange that time at Mr. Wilder's convenience, of course. He must always be your first priority."

Luke retraced his steps back to the entrance hall. "Here we are." He opened a door that was almost concealed in the wood paneling and made Rowan wonder if there were other secret places in the house. It was certainly old enough. Luke's office was immaculate. He took a seat behind an expansive, leather-topped desk, pulling out a folder from a drawer. He didn't invite Rowan to sit so he stood with his hands clasped behind his back to keep from fidgeting.

"A few ground rules first," Luke said. "You will address Mr. Wilder as Sir unless he instructs you otherwise. You can call me Mr. Redding and the chef, who I'll introduce you to later, is Mr. Halvorsen. You've already met Rayne and first names are fine with the rest of the staff—that's Benjy and Frank in the kitchen, the cleaning crew and groundsmen, though you won't come across them often. The only people entitled to give you orders are the client, me and, in my absence, Mr. Halvorsen. He acts as my deputy when I'm not here. Is that clear?"

"Yes, Mr. Redding."

"Good. Now, your meal times will be by agreement with Mr. Wilder. He may want you to join him, or he may prefer that you serve him and eat separately. If that's the case, he will be aware that he has to give you time to take meals. Your working day will start at whatever time he needs you and finish when he's done with you. If he wants you with him overnight, that's his prerogative." Luke paused, steepling his fingers in front of him. "You've read the contract. Outside of it, it is up to you what you do with the client but, be assured, you are under no obligation to have sex with him. This is not a brothel."

Rowan nodded his understanding.

"If you feel pressured in any way, you are to come to me immediately and I will deal with the situation."

"Thank you," Rowan said. "I appreciate that." He sincerely hoped he would never have cause to need his boss for that reason. "Um… There was something in the contract about oral contact. I agreed to that."

"You did. I have Mr. Wilder's medical certification on file and he has seen yours. You are still within your rights to request the use of a condom if that's what you prefer. I'd like to reassure you that Mr. Wilder has an impeccable reputation as a Dominant." He leafed through the pile of papers from the folder. "Is there anything you would like to change?"

"No, thank you. I went over everything very carefully before I signed the contract and I don't want to change my mind."

Luke smiled. "Well, you'll have the opportunity to review the paperwork before each new client arrives. And remember, I'm here for you as well as him. If anything, anything at all, worries or bothers you, come straight to me."

Luke's absolute certainty in his role eased some of the butterflies in Rowan's stomach. Luke Redding seemed like a man that kept his word.

It was another half an hour before Luke finished taking Rowan through the various rules and regulations of The Retreat and Rowan's head was buzzing by the time he was done.

"Don't worry if you don't remember everything I've told you," Luke said, humor in his tone. "You will learn as you go along, and I'm here to correct you if you go wrong. Punishments, however, will be Mr. Wilder's domain."

Rowan caught the sparkle in Luke's eyes and had to repress a smile. Luke was a Dominant first, manager second, and clearly relished the idea of administering punishment. Rowan was relieved he would only have to deal with one Dom at a time. He decided staying silent was the best course of action.

"I'll give you the rest of the tour now," Luke said, pushing his chair back. "Then you can explore on your own for a bit and I'll meet you in the staff dining room for lunch. It's just off the kitchen."

Luke led the way back to the entrance hall then ascended the left-hand staircase to the landing. "The bedrooms don't have nameplates or numbers, but they each have a color theme so that's how the staff recognize them. Mr. Wilder may choose to use one of them, or all of them, during his stay. That's entirely up to him and each room has its...surprises. Those I'll leave you to discover for yourself. Each room has its own bathroom and a phone that can connect you either to my office or the kitchen. Catering is available twenty-four hours a day, as am I. When I'm not in my office, the number will reroute to my mobile so you can always get hold of me if you need to. Don't ever worry about disturbing me. That's what I'm here for." Luke pushed open the first bedroom door then gestured for Rowan to step inside. Rowan's jaw dropped.

"This must be the Blue Room. It's fabulous." He gazed at the luxurious furnishings, which included a magnificent four-poster. Every detail was exquisite. He remembered Olly mentioning a sling hidden in the canopy of a four-poster and wondered if this was the same one.

"Mr. Hoffman and his partner have spared no expense in giving The Retreat the best of everything.

Each room is unique and the furniture is either bespoke or antique. One of your duties will be to take care of the cleaning in whichever room Mr. Wilder selects for his own use. We have a cleaning service on call and they will attend to the rest of the house but only when Mr. Wilder is not in residence, or at night after he has retired. They will do a more thorough clean at the end of each guest's stay. We don't want our clients to be bothered by mundane necessities and aim to keep housekeeping as invisible as possible. You will also be responsible for refreshing the bed linen and towels, but not for the laundry. We have another service for that. I'll show you where the sheets and towels are stored later. Is that clear?"

"Yes, Mr. Redding. May I ask if you have specialist cleaning products and polish?" Rowan ran his fingers over the arm of a particularly fine chair. "I wouldn't want to be using a can of Pledge on this furniture."

Luke chuckled. "I think we have everything you could possibly need but if there is a particular product you think would be better, let me know and I'll make sure it's brought in for you."

The remaining four rooms were all equally stunning, though Rowan harbored a secret preference for the Blue Room. Any of them would be a pleasure to look after and he could almost smell beeswax and linseed oil. He just hoped he could avoid breaking anything because he would have to work for free for the rest of his life to pay for any replacements.

The tour continued downstairs. Rowan tried hard to memorize the circuitous routes between the dining hall, snug, formal lounge and the recreation facilities. There was a well-equipped gym and a sizeable pool, sauna and steam room all housed in a separate block that was modern but had been built to blend seamlessly with the house. Luke also showed him the stairs that led to the attic and told him they would explore there shortly.

"Now I'll introduce you to one of the highlights of The Retreat."

Rowan didn't hide his curiosity. He wasn't sure how the facilities could get any better.

Inside the cozy, wood-paneled snug, Luke pressed one of the panels to reveal a concealed door. He closed it again so that Rowan could see how cleverly it was hidden. With the door shut it was completely invisible. Even though Rowan knew it was there, he couldn't make out its edges. Luke opened it again and beyond the door a set of steps led downward.

"You may be surprised to learn that this doesn't lead to the wine cellar," Luke said. "That's accessed via the kitchen." He reached the bottom of the steps and flicked a switch, illuminating a cavernous space. "This is a genuine dungeon, though the equipment is a lot safer than the devices that would have been used here centuries ago."

Rowan stared. He realized that he wasn't looking at a single room because along one wall were three further doors with small barred windows set into them. He walked over to peer through one of them and found a cell, equipped with a chair that he imagined might be used by a psychopathic dentist. He gulped. All kinds of kinky scenarios ran through his mind. A quick peek into the other two cells revealed different set-ups. One had a bare floor and several sets of chains attached to the walls, the other contained some kind of frame that he couldn't imagine a use for.

The main area of the dungeon housed a selection of impressive equipment including a leather-padded cross, a spanking bench and a cage large enough for a man to stand in. There were several storage chests and cupboards but Rowan hardly dared look to see what was inside them. His heart was pounding and his skin felt hot, almost fevered. His cock was doing its best impression of a steel rod. He caught Luke's eye and his cheeks burned as much as the rest of him.

"It's... Well, I've never seen anything like it. It's wonderful. The closest I've come to anything like this is when I toured the private rooms at The Underground."

"Some of the equipment may well be familiar. Mr. Hoffman used the same manufacturer that produces all the kit for his club."

Rowan nodded. It made sense. Carey Hoffman didn't stint on anything where The Underground was concerned. Why would he do it here at The Retreat? Rowan really hoped that Mr. Wilder would be keen to test out the dungeon's facilities. He'd have to keep his enthusiasm in check though because it wouldn't be up to him.

"Now you know where the door is, you can come back later and explore more on your own if you want to," Luke said. "But now we have to get to the top of the house so I can show you the attic."

To Rowan's surprise, the attic was almost as inspiring to his imagination as the dungeon. It wasn't full of equipment but at one gable end there was a huge picture window with an incredible view of the forest. Perfectly positioned in front of it, as if it had been designed that way, an A-frame constructed from ancient oak beams supported the roof. Cast iron D-rings were set into the wood at strategic points and it wasn't hard for Rowan to visualize how a man could be restrained there. He wondered if the distraction of the view would reduce the pain of a flogging, or the burn of a whip.

Once they were back in the entrance hall, Luke gave Rowan directions to the kitchen. "I'll meet you there shortly. I have one or two phone calls to make first, but lunch will be ready so introduce yourself to Tor and he'll make sure you're fed."

Rowan wandered back to the kitchen in a daze, his head full of the possibilities that The Retreat offered. His slight trepidation at meeting Mr. Wilder the next day had been replaced by anticipation. Rowan loved everything he had seen so far and he knew he'd made the right career choice.

Chapter Four

"Mr. Wilder! Mr. Wilder, are you in there?" The persistent knocking on his office door told Lorcan Wilder that he wasn't going to be left in peace anytime soon.

"Come in, Drew." Lorcan stepped away from the floor-to-ceiling window and its view of the Golden Gate Bridge. He faced the door, which swung open to reveal his harried personal assistant. Andrew Gates, fresh out of college, shiny MBA in his back pocket, was flushed and his normally immaculate hair tousled.

"People are looking for you, sir. The press office wants another statement and the phones are ringing off the hook."

"Let them ring."

"Sir?"

"Drew, the sale of this company has been planned for months. Every scenario has been worked through. Press releases prepared. The staff informed, right down to the night janitor. Everybody knows what they need to know."

"Yes, sir. Of course. But you haven't said what you're going to do next or where you're going."

"No, I haven't." Lorcan smiled. "And I'm not going to. My life is my own now. It doesn't belong to the Board, the shareholders or the media, despite what they might think. My plans are my business, no one else's, and I've gone to great lengths to minimize press intrusion." He used the same tone he employed when speaking to his Board of Directors—firm and calm. Drew's shoulders slumped. He was cute, eminently fuckable and certainly submissive, but Lorcan didn't play with his staff, however much of a crush they might have on him.

"You've done a great job for me and the new CEO is lucky to have you at his beck and call, Drew. Please go back to the boardroom and tell them I'll be with them in fifteen minutes."

"Yes, sir." Drew scurried from the room, leaving Lorcan alone. He surveyed his office one final time then took his jacket from the back of his chair. He slipped it on, checked his pocket for his keys then left, closing the door behind him. At nine in the evening, his outer office was empty. He made it to the service elevator without running across anyone and from there it was a quick trip to the basement garage. The security cameras would capture his E-Type as he left but there was nothing anyone could do to stop him. Sooner or later the directors would realize he wasn't coming back. He didn't enjoy lying to Drew but on this occasion, it was justified and Lorcan wouldn't be the one dealing with rabid journalists demanding information.

Heels tapping on the concrete, Lorcan crossed the garage to his reserved space. He hadn't driven himself for several years and was looking forward to getting behind the wheel. His chauffeur now served another man. Lorcan would miss Dalton's acerbic wit and lack of deference. He'd left him a generous parting gift — one he would find when checking the glove compartment of the company BMW. Drew's parting gift would also be waiting for him when he got home. Lorcan hoped Drew wouldn't be too upset at his departure but he was young and ambitious — he'd get over it and find a new mentor to crush on.

The scent of leather surrounded him as Lorcan sank into the Jaguar's driver's seat. He shut the door and for a moment enjoyed the cocoon of silence. The tinted windows with their armored glass provided both protection and privacy, though Lorcan often spurned the first and craved the second. He gripped the leather-wrapped steering wheel until his knuckles blanched. Letting go was harder than he'd thought it would be. Work, the business he'd built from scratch, had been his entire life since he was nineteen. Ten years on, it was time to be selfish. He had more money than the treasury of a small country and intended to enjoy it whilst deciding what he wanted to do next. Self-indulgence would be his mantra while he shucked off years of stress. Spontaneity, however, was not his thing. He had a plan. A detailed blueprint for the coming weeks that had been months in the making.

Lorcan flexed his fingers, imagining the handle of a crop in his palm instead of the wheel. He could hear the hiss as his strike split the air and the smack of leather on willing flesh. Beneath the fine wool of his Armani suit pants and the silk-cotton blend of his underwear, his dick twitched. With a wry grin, he inserted the key into the ignition. The car's marque was appropriate because the purr of the engine could have belonged to a sleek big cat. Lorcan caressed the gear knob before putting the car into first. He'd chosen a stick shift model because, as in every aspect of his life, he had to be in complete control.

The drive from Lorcan's office building on Mission Street to his home in Pacific Heights was less than four miles but he took his time, and a circuitous route, in getting there. Automatic number plate recognition ensured he had only a brief wait while his electronic gates opened. A remote gave him access to the four-car garage and, once the Jag was parked, he felt able to relax a fraction. An interior door took him into the house where he followed a familiar path through the kitchen to the hall. A spiral staircase led to his expansive bedroom. He loved the house and the privacy it afforded him, but he wasn't sorry to be leaving it for a while. Two suitcases, already packed, stood in front of the fitted cupboards in the bedroom.

He stripped with his usual economy of movement, pausing to examine his reflection in a full-length mirror — not through vanity but in a clinical appraisal of his physique. His job hadn't allowed him much time for exercise but he'd done his best to stay in shape. The defined abs and flat belly were a testament to his stubborn will more than anything. He gave a brief nod of satisfaction then headed for the attached bathroom. After a sixteen-hour working day, a hot shower was top of his current agenda. Before he could turn on the spray, his phone rang. He retrieved it from his jacket pocket only because he recognized the ring tone as unique to his best friend, Giles Greville.

"Giles, I'm naked. This had better be good." Lorcan leaned against the bathroom doorframe.

"If only you were a sweet, young, spankable blond. I'd be there in an instant." Giles chuckled.

"With your voracious appetites, I'd be shocked if there was a single man left in the city you haven't had your wicked way with, blond or not."

"While you, of course, are much more discerning. Or perhaps it's just harder to find pretty things prepared to give in to your…unique demands."

"I'm hardly unique, Giles."

"True. There are a fair number of kinky bastards in this town, myself among them. How did it go today?"

"As planned." Lorcan rolled his head from side to side, easing some knots from his neck.

"As if you'd allow it to happen any other way. My friend, the ultimate control freak."

"Have I ever denied it?"

"So, now you've risen from the realms of the super-rich to the stratospherically wealthy, how do you feel?"

Lorcan considered for a moment. "Liberated. My time is my own."

"And mine is taken up with fielding all the calls you re-routed my way. I'm surprised you have an ounce of sanity left, Lorc."

"I owe you. I don't want anyone to know where I'm going. No interruptions."

"Your secret is safe with me. I'm green with envy, however, and will be expecting detailed reports on all the facilities. If the place weren't booked out for the next two years, I'd be treating you as my advance research party. As it is, I've had to join a damned waiting list."

"I'm there for a month, Giles. If you want to join me for a few days…well, the invitation is open."

"I don't want to rain on your parade, but I may well be tempted. Dad confiscated my passport after that last episode in Paris but I know the combination to the safe."

Lorcan laughed. Giles always managed to entertain him. "Can I get in the shower now?"

"Oh…yes. I was just checking in. What time are you flying out in the morning?"

"Eleven. The advantage of a private jet is how civilized the flight times can be."

"That sure is the truth. Happy travels, my friend, and don't do anything I wouldn't."

"That leaves very little. I'll be in touch, Giles." Lorcan turned off the phone before tossing it onto the bed. He had no intention of taking any more calls that night.

The shower was less about getting clean than washing away the past. Water and scented gel worked their magic. Lorcan had always been able to compartmentalize parts of his life—it was a survival strategy. Now he locked one of those compartments for good. He was proud of what he'd achieved in the business world, but work had taken over his life to such an extent that he had lost his sense of self. He wanted that back.

Stepping from beneath the spray, Lorcan dug his toes into the bath mat. He fancied he could feel every strand of the pile caressing the soles of his feet. Senses dulled by years of stress could finally come alive again. He gave a wry chuckle at his own fanciful musing.

"Get a grip, Wilder. No one's gonna want an overly sensitive Dom spanking his ass." He toweled dry then went to bed, even though it was still early for him. The thread count of his sheets ran to four figures and for once he was able to appreciate cotton that could have been silk it was so smooth. Propping himself against duck-down pillows, he settled his computer on his lap. The webpage he wanted was bookmarked so it took seconds to bring up the online brochure for The Retreat. If it had been a paper version, it would have been well-thumbed from frequent reading. As it was, it had the benefit of pristine, electronic pages. Lorcan had an eidetic memory so he didn't need to read the pages at all but somehow it was more exciting to examine the words and pictures on the screen than to recall them.

"The Retreat is a haven from the world, where you can be yourself, where dreams become reality." Reading the words aloud gave them solidity. "I can't wait." *And now I don't have to. Not for much longer.* The day he had received an email containing a link to The Retreat's hidden website had been the day his life had changed. It was a catalyst, a spark, and all he'd needed to take steps that had been forming in his mind for two years. Maintaining his expensive membership of The Underground when he only got to the UK once or twice a year had been self-indulgent, but his years of loyal membership had paid off. Only a very select elite got to hear about The Retreat. It was an endorsement of his status as a respected Dominant and demonstrated a level of trust he had no right to expect. He had met Carey Hoffman, The Underground's charismatic owner, several times and he liked him a great deal. Carey exuded calm and doted on his submissive, Alastair, but beneath his serene surface was a shrewd, ruthless businessman — qualities Lorcan admired.

He scanned the rest of the familiar text, which covered the history of the period building that housed

The Retreat, gave a few details of the surrounding area and its attractions and included pictures of beautifully appointed rooms that married antique fittings with modern comforts. Each room had hidden secrets, designed with the discerning Dom in mind. Bed canopies concealed slings, innocuous furniture had been converted to tools designed to torment, and cages were revealed behind hidden panels and trapdoors. The possibilities for play were endless. Every possible kink was catered for.

Once he'd secured his reservation, Lorcan had been able to specify all kinds of tantalizing details—the staff who would attend to his needs, what they would wear and be expected to do. Menus had been provided for everything from the ordinary—food and drink—to the intriguing—toys and tools, costumes and equipment. He had been able to select each detail personally down to the type of condom he preferred, flavors of lube and the scent of toiletries. He felt pampered before he had even arrived. Reading through everything again brought his cock to life, but he didn't touch. Denial would put him in the right frame of mind for his arrival at The Retreat. He closed his laptop. Feeling a bit like a small boy on Christmas Eve, he wanted to sleep so that the morning would come quicker and, after his browsing session, his dreams promised to be stimulating. He hoped the nightmares that still haunted him would stay away.

* * * *

Flying wasn't one of Lorcan's favorite activities, even in the comfort of a private jet. He always felt a bit claustrophobic. Snoozing, memorizing British vocabulary, watching movies and snacking on food provided by the deferential cabin stewardess passed the time but he was still relieved when the plane touched down on British soil. He disembarked and made it through passport control with the ease of privilege and he was grateful for it. After twelve hours in the air, he was tired. At home, it was late at night but in the UK, the new day hadn't long started.

The uniformed chauffeur waiting in the arrivals hall held a card with 'The Retreat' written on it. Lorcan smiled. He was the only passenger so it was hardly necessary but for the avoidance of doubt, he introduced himself.

"Lorcan Wilder. I assume you're my ride."

"Yes! Yes, sir. I love your accent. I'm Rayne and I'll be your driver for the duration of your stay. I have your bags, so as soon as you're ready, we can go."

Lorcan half listened as Rayne chattered all the way from the airport terminal to the car. He was cute, his uniform tailored to show off his slim figure. Even his cap sat at a jaunty angle. Lorcan wondered if it was permissible to make him drive wearing a ball gag. He guessed not. There was probably some archaic English law against it. He settled into the back seat of the car, grateful for the tinted windows and dim lighting.

"Sir, you'll find ice and drinks in the center armrest," Rayne said. "Please help yourself. The drive will take less than two hours so please relax. We'll be there before you know it."

Lorcan poured himself water from a bottle declaring itself to be from a Welsh spring in the mountains, adding a few cubes of ice to the lead crystal glass. He ignored the chocolates and nuts. Rayne's driving was so smooth Lorcan's drink barely rippled as they sped along country roads. He sipped steadily, fending off the dehydration caused by the long flight. Drinking also eased the headache building behind his eyes and he was able to take a bit more notice of his surroundings. The countryside was very different from home. The amount of green was overwhelming and everything seemed rooted in hundreds of years of history. There wasn't a whole lot of thatch in San Francisco. He slid the window down an inch. Even the air tasted green somehow. Lorcan massaged the back of his neck with his free hand in an attempt to reduce the tension in his muscles. He hoped the beds at The Retreat were as comfortable as they looked in the pictures because he fully intended to test one of them out as soon as he arrived. With no demands on him, he could let his body adjust to the new time zone gradually rather than force himself to stay awake and be miserable for the rest of the day.

He let his mind drift into one of his favorite fantasies. Predicament bondage challenged his creative brain and his imagination was particularly good at conjuring up all kinds of wicked scenarios. He had requested just one personal submissive at The Retreat and Carey Hoffman had assured him that the young man who had been selected fitted his requirements perfectly. Lorcan couldn't wait to meet him. He must have drifted into a half-doze because the next thing he knew, Rayne was opening the car door.

"Mr. Wilder? We're here, sir."

Lorcan blinked, the outside light too bright for his tired eyes. "Already? That was quick." He got out of the car before indulging in a luxurious stretch, making a couple of his vertebrae pop. The action was followed by a yawn he couldn't stop.

"You need to catch up on your sleep, sir," Rayne said as he heaved Lorcan's bags from the trunk. *Boot, it's a boot over here.*

"About ten years' worth," he replied. He stared at the building that would be his home for the next month. "This could feature in a scene from *Gormenghast*," he mused, admiring the tangle of towers and arches. The place certainly had character. He was too tired to take it in properly but resolved to explore once he had rested.

"Follow me, sir," Rayne prompted. "I'll take your bags into the entrance hall." As Rayne approached the impressive front door, it swung open. Lorcan felt a rush of new energy as he took in the sight before him. He caught Rayne's cheeky grin and gave him a light cuff in reprimand. Rayne lowered his eyes but Lorcan wasn't fooled by the show of submission. He made a mental note to keep an eye on the brat. He put Rayne out of his mind and focused on the vision in front of him. A young man, blond head bowed, knelt in the center of the hall. Wearing nothing but underwear, he sat on his heels with his knees parted, hands clasped behind his back. Lorcan circled him, taking slow, measured steps, examining his slender body and lightly defined muscles. Carey Hoffman had chosen well.

Lorcan gave the blond head a gentle touch, letting the young man register his presence. He detected the slightest shiver and protectiveness surged through him. He blinked, shocked at his own extreme reaction.

"I see you've met Rowan."

Lorcan tore his eyes away from the kneeling sub, irritated at the distraction.

"I apologize for disturbing you. I'm Luke Redding, general manager here at The Retreat. It's a pleasure to meet you, Mr. Wilder. We can catch up later after you and Rowan get acquainted." Luke dismissed Rayne with a flick of his fingers, then retreated to what Lorcan assumed was his office. It must have been Luke who'd opened the main door but Lorcan had been captivated by a kneeling sub and hadn't noticed him. He was impressed by Luke's insight into the situation. He could only be another Dominant, able to recognize Lorcan's need to connect with a new submissive.

Left alone with Rowan in the grand entrance hall, Lorcan took a slow breath. He wanted to make the right first impression. He stood two paces in front of Rowan's knees and assumed a relaxed stance with his hands loosely clasped behind his back.

"This floor can't be comfortable on your knees, Rowan. Please stand."

Rowan rose with unstudied grace. His head remained bowed but Lorcan wanted to see his face.

"Look at me. You may speak."

Rowan made eye contact and Lorcan suppressed a sigh of pleasure. The young man was beautiful. His clear blue eyes shone with intelligence and his lips promised the softest of kisses. There was a hint of gold in his hair that drew Lorcan's gaze.

"Are you cold?" Rowan wore only a pair of black mesh shorts. The effect was tantalizing, with the ridge of his cock clearly visible but still concealed. The rear of the scanty garment was cut away to expose two perfect ass cheeks, separated by the narrowest strip of fabric.

"No, Sir. I'm quite comfortable, thank you." Rowan's voice was soft but melodic.

"Then perhaps you could show me to my room."

"There are five bedrooms at your disposal, Sir," Rowan said. "They've all been prepared for you. I only arrived yesterday, but the owners had a whole team of people in last week getting everything ready. I can show you all of them, if you'd like me to."

Lorcan fought back a yawn. "For now, take me to the one that you like the most. I need to take a nap, so all I want is a comfortable bed. You can give me the tour later."

"I've never traveled long-haul, Sir, so I can only imagine what jet lag must feel like."

Lorcan was pleased that Rowan felt comfortable enough to speak without prompting. "It sucks. Big time." This time the yawn escaped before Lorcan could stop it.

"Follow me, Sir. The Blue Room is particularly beautiful."

Tracking Rowan up the sweeping staircase proved to be an inspiring experience. He had an ass that Lorcan could quite happily watch for hours. Once inside the room, Rowan immediately went to the bed and folded back the covers.

"The bathroom is just through that door, Sir. If it's okay, I'll fetch your bags while you freshen up."

Lorcan nodded. "Go ahead. Make two journeys if you need to."

Rowan slipped from the room and Lorcan immediately missed his presence. He shook his head. "I'm doomed."

In the bathroom, he splashed cold water on his face then used the toilet. A shower would have to wait, though it was tempting. He'd probably pass out and end up drowning in an inch of water. That would be a tragedy because it would mean he couldn't get to know Rowan better.

Lorcan stripped, throwing his clothes in the general direction of a chair. The bed proved to be as comfortable as it looked and as his head sank into the pillows, the world faded away.

Rowan recognized the incongruity of hauling luggage in his underwear. In fact, the idea that what he was wearing constituted underwear was something of a joke, there was so little of it. He pushed open the door of the Blue Room to find Lorcan Wilder already asleep in the bed. Lorcan lay on his side, the covers pulled up to his hip leaving his bare arse exposed. Rowan admired the lean lines of Lorcan's muscled body and wondered what it would be like to trace the dips and curves with his tongue. He shook his head. He should be focusing on his job, not acting like a voyeur.

He maneuvered Lorcan's bags inside from the landing as quietly as he could. The room was flooded with light so he closed the heavy drapes, casting the bed in deep shadow. Moving silently on bare feet, he gathered Lorcan's discarded clothes for the laundry. Then, after giving the bathroom a quick check and re-folding the towels, Rowan slipped away. He used the laundry chute, knowing that the clothes would be expertly cleaned and pressed within twenty-four hours. After that, he made his way to his own room where he pulled on comfortable jeans and a loose T-shirt. He checked the time and, seeing that Ed would likely be between shifts, dialed his number. He made himself comfortable on the bed and waited for the call to connect.

"Rowan! Is that you? Is he there yet, your mystery man? Tell me everything. How's it going? Has he tied you up yet?"

Rowan giggled. "I'm fine, thank you, Ed. Yes, he has arrived, but he's sleeping. Jet lag. He's an American."

"I need more than that," Ed declared. "Give me a blow by blow account of your day. I want every detail."

After plumping his pillows and settling back against them, Rowan closed his eyes. "Well, I didn't sleep very well because I was nervous and excited. Rayne left for the airport at the crack of dawn then Luke, Mr. Redding, called me into his office after breakfast."

"He's your boss, right?"

"Yes, I told you about him last night when I rang. Were you not listening?"

"Of course I was! I just tune out the boring bits. Not enough room in my brain."

"Anyway, he handed me a package and told me that it was what I needed to wear for when Mr Wilder arrived. He told me that I'd be expected to be waiting in the entrance hall, kneeling. Then he sent me back to my room to get ready."

"So what did you have to wear? I'd bet good money that it was made of rubber or leather."

"That's a bet you'd lose then." Rowan laughed. "Picture a pair of the shortest shorts you've ever seen, backless and made of some kind of net fabric. That was it. That was all I was given to wear."

"My God! That sounds…hot!"

"You're not supposed to say that," Rowan said. "You're supposed to express your shock then provide sympathy for my plight."

"I can picture you on your knees, virtually naked. You probably daydream about being in that kind of situation all the time. That job really is a dream come true for you, isn't it?"

"You know me too well." Rowan sighed. "He's gorgeous, Ed. I'm not sure what I was expecting but it wasn't tall, dark and lickable. He looks young, too. I mean, I know he's not thirty yet but he looks younger than he is. I've only spent a few minutes in his company so far but he has this kind of aura of restrained power. It's hard to describe, but I can easily imagine him taking charge in the boardroom."

"So you'll let him fuck you then?"

Rowan let his mind drift into a scene where Lorcan had him tied over a spanking bench, spread and prepped. He could imagine the aching need to be filled.

"That'll be his decision," he said. "It's not part of the contract, but can be negotiated between us if that's what he wants."

"You will." Ed sounded smug in his certainty. "And I don't blame you if he's as hot as you say he is."

"He could still turn out to be a complete arsehole," Rowan mused. "I'm hardly in a position to make a judgment just yet." He picked up Bilbo and gave him a cuddle. "But he hasn't done anything so far to make me think that."

"I have to go," Ed said. "But you have to ring me again tonight with an update."

"If I can, I will. I'm not promising though. This job is going to be a bit unpredictable. I don't have set hours or anything and the client's body clock is going to be a bit skewed for a while."

"I wish you could tell me his name, it's weird calling him 'the client'. I think I'll pick a name for him. How about Cyril?"

Rowan laughed. "No. That's just wrong. Have a good day, Ed. I'll talk to you again as soon as I can." He disconnected the call. Hugging Bilbo close, he picked up his Kindle, deciding to read for a while. He'd go and check on Lorcan in a couple of hours. It wouldn't do to let him sleep too long but as he hadn't had any instructions he'd just have to go on instinct. He placed a quick call to the kitchen, ordering a light snack of sliced fruits, cheese and biscuits to be ready for him to collect later. Satisfied that he'd done everything he needed to, Rowan immersed himself in his spy thriller. Secretly, he thought his new life was far more exciting than the plot of the book.

Chapter Five

Rowan tried to read but found it impossible to concentrate. He didn't want Lorcan to wake up alone on his first day in a strange place. After an hour of reading the same page over and over again, he gave up. He took off his top and jeans then made his way back to the Blue Room. He slipped inside, letting his eyes adjust to the dim light. Lorcan was in the same position that Rowan had seen him in an hour before. He didn't stir. Rowan sank to his knees, got as comfortable as he could and prepared to wait.

It was no hardship to have time to think. Lorcan had made a good first impression. He made Rowan nervous, but in a good way — the kind of nervous that heated his skin and stiffened his cock. He let his mind wander into daydreams that had inspired him since he was old enough to understand what submission was.

He was alert to every twitch from the direction of the bed as if a corner of his brain was reserved for Lorcan, so when Lorcan mumbled in his sleep Rowan's fantasies were relegated to the back of his mind. He edged a little closer. Lorcan's words were incoherent but whatever was disturbing him wasn't enjoyable. Frown lines creased his forehead and there was a sheen of perspiration on his skin. His head jerked from one side to the other and the mumbling grew louder. Rowan could make out the word 'no', repeated over and over. He rose from his knees then grasped Lorcan's shoulder in the hope that his touch might be calming. Instead, Lorcan's arm flew up and he caught Rowan's cheek with the back of his hand. It wasn't a hard blow but enough to make Rowan yelp. Lorcan's eyes flickered open.

"You were having a nightmare, Sir," Rowan said. "I'm sorry I disturbed you."

Lorcan's eyes narrowed. "There's a red mark on your face. Did I hit you?" He sat up, his expression concerned.

"You were asleep. You didn't know what you were doing. It's nothing."

"That's for me to decide. Is there any ice around here?"

"Yes, Sir. I filled the bucket on the dresser earlier today."

Lorcan got out of bed, apparently unconcerned about his nudity. He fetched a towel from the bathroom before collecting the ice bucket from the dresser. Bringing both to the bed, he tipped a quantity of ice cubes into the towel then twisted the ends to make a loose bundle. "Sit here." He patted the side of the bed. Rowan perched on the edge of the mattress and Lorcan pressed the cold towel to his face.

"I'm so sorry. I should have warned you about the nightmares. I'm mortified that you got hurt, even accidentally."

Rowan wasn't sure what to say. Lorcan wanted to blame himself and there wasn't much that Rowan could do or say to change his mind, so he accepted the ice treatment with as much grace as he could muster. He fixed his gaze on Lorcan's abs, resisting the urge to peek lower.

"Luke Redding will take a bullwhip to my arse for this," Lorcan said.

"I'd much rather you took one to mine," Rowan whispered.

"Hmm. Seems like I have a pain slut on my hands." Lorcan lifted the towel, peering beneath it. He pressed his fingers to Rowan's cheek. "Does that hurt?"

Rowan didn't want to answer because either way Lorcan would stop touching him. He settled for shaking his head.

"Use words, please. And tell the truth because I'll know if you lie to me."

"It's a little sore, Sir," Rowan admitted. "But I can hardly feel it. It's nothing, I promise."

"Okay, but I want you to tell me if the pain gets any worse and hold the ice there a bit longer. It'll reduce the swelling."

Lorcan stood with his hands on his hips, feet a shoulder width apart, his stare intense. Rowan wanted to fidget but managed to stay still with an effort.

"This wasn't how I pictured us getting to know each other," Lorcan said. "Candlelight, you kneeling naked at my side accepting treats from my fingers, then a spanking so my hand could get familiar with your arse. That's how it was supposed to be." Lorcan's gaze strayed toward Rowan's groin. "I can see the idea appeals to you."

Rowan would have liked to relocate the towel full of ice from his cheek to his rigid cock. He groaned and, from the heat in his face, knew he must be blushing.

"I think we should start again. There's no need to give up on the plan. I'm going to take a shower." Lorcan plumped the pillows. "You get into the bed and stay put. Keep the ice on your face."

Rowan obeyed, swinging his legs up onto the mattress. Lorcan pulled the covers over him.

"I won't be long. Try to relax."

Lorcan disappeared into the bathroom and Rowan sank back against pillows that smelled of lemons. He was so hard, he ached. He allowed his free hand to stray toward his cock. Lorcan poked his head out of the bathroom.

"No touching." He grinned then retreated.

"Damn," Rowan whispered. "How did he know?" He sat on his free hand and pressed the ice harder against his face. The cold was a convenient distraction. He had no doubt that Lorcan would follow through with his plans, which fulfilled some of the fantasies that Rowan had been dreaming about not long before. His arse clenched as he imagined Lorcan's palm making contact with his sensitive flesh. He wondered if Lorcan would let him come. Rowan wasn't religious but he would pray if it meant finding release.

The sound of the shower ceased and he could hear Lorcan whistling as he dried off. A few minutes later he emerged from the bathroom, still naked. He seemed unselfconscious about his body and Rowan could understand why. Lorcan took care of himself, that much was clear. It took effort not to drool as Rowan got a perfect view of Lorcan's backside when he strolled across the room to his suitcases. He unzipped one of them then rummaged through the contents.

"I think I should be appropriately dressed for our introduction, don't you?"

Rowan eyed the leather trousers dangling from Lorcan's hand and nodded his approval with a bit too much enthusiasm. "Yes, Sir."

Lorcan pulled the trousers up his legs before zipping the fly closed. The garment hugged his shape and hung from his hips. Rowan could see traces of trimmed stubble above the waistband. Knowing that Lorcan was bare beneath the leather made him all the more alluring.

"Now, how do we go about getting some food in this place?"

"Sir, I took the liberty of arranging some light snacks for you. If I may, I'll ring the kitchen and have them brought up."

"Perfect," Lorcan said. "Can you have them bring some juice as well? Apple if they have it."

Rowan put his towel full of ice down before reaching for the phone on the bedside table. He dialed the kitchen, relayed his request then set the receiver back on the stand. "I should get rid of this ice, Sir." He waited for Lorcan's permission to get out of bed.

"Yes, go ahead. I'll take another look at your cheek later. I'm sure Luke will have a proper ice pack if we need one." Lorcan opened the drapes and the room flooded with light. Rowan had lost track of the time but guessed it was early afternoon. He slipped into the bathroom, dumped the ice into the sink then hung the towel behind the door. Back in the bedroom, Lorcan was seated at the small table in front of the window. He had placed a pillow on the floor at his side.

"Take off your underwear, Rowan," he ordered.

Rowan rolled the flimsy garment down his legs and stepped out of it. He clasped his hands behind his back, ignoring the bounce of his rigid dick.

"You have a beautiful body. I wonder how well you can control it." Lorcan crossed his ankles, completely relaxed. "You are not to come without my permission, do you understand?"

"Yes, Sir." Rowan understood—he wasn't sure he could obey.

There was a soft tap at the door and Lorcan gestured that Rowan should answer it. One of Luke's kitchen assistants stood outside with a covered tray. He didn't bat an eyelid at Rowan's nudity, just asked where he should put the tray.

"On the table next to me here," Lorcan said. "What's your name?"

"Frank, sir."

"Thank you for bringing the tray up, Frank. Could you relay a message to the chef for me?"

"Of course, sir."

"I'd like dinner at seven. I don't mind where it's served but somewhere cozy would be nice."

"And the menu, sir?"

"I believe the chef has a list of my likes and dislikes. I'm happy to leave the menu up to him."

Frank grinned. "He'll be very pleased to hear that, sir." He scampered from the room, pulling the door closed behind him.

"I think I just found the way to our chef's heart," Lorcan said. He took the pristine white cloth from the top of the tray to reveal a jug of cloudy apple juice and two tumblers, a marble slab piled with miniature samples of a variety of cheeses, a plate of sliced fruits and a selection of crackers. "This looks delicious. Your choice?" he asked Rowan.

"I wasn't sure how hungry you'd be," Rowan said. "So I went for something light. I hope that's okay—I can always order more later on."

"I don't tend to eat much in the middle of the day," Lorcan said. "This is perfect. Why don't you pour us both a glass of juice then come and kneel next to me."

Rowan did as he was asked, leaving his own glass of juice on the tray. He knelt on the pillow next to Lorcan's chair.

"Is there anything here that you don't like, Rowan?" Lorcan asked.

"I'm not fond of blue cheese, Sir," Rowan admitted, "but I like everything else."

Lorcan sliced off a section of brie, loaded it onto a cracker then held it to Rowan's lips. Rowan ate the tempting morsel.

"The underwear you were wearing was my choice. However, I think I prefer you naked. I confess to a penchant for kinky briefs but most of my pleasure comes from removing them." Lorcan leaned down and took a firm hold of Rowan's rigid shaft. "I will have to do something about this though."

Rowan made a garbled sound through clenched teeth. He was going to come all over Lorcan's hand and there was nothing he could do about it. He gasped as an orgasm rolled through his body and jerked, unable to control his reaction to Lorcan's touch.

"I'm sorry! I'm sorry…" He panted his apology.

"I'm not." Lorcan licked a finger. "You taste good."

"Oh God." Rowan found it difficult to keep his back straight.

"I don't think He had much to do with it, do you?" Lorcan went to the bathroom and came back with a damp flannel. He cleaned his hand then applied the cloth to Rowan's flagging dick. "Once we're done eating, I have a chastity device with your name on it. In the meantime, I seem to have developed an appetite." He discarded the flannel then pressed a grape to Rowan's lips before eating several himself.

Rowan ate everything Lorcan offered him but found it difficult to concentrate on the food while picturing various forms of chastity. Just the idea of Lorcan having absolute control over his body made Rowan shiver — in a good way. If Lorcan noticed his distraction, he didn't mention it but Rowan fancied there was a certain smugness in the curve of Lorcan's lips. To his utter horror, Rowan's dick began to harden again. He gave it a miserable glance, willing it to subside, but then Lorcan stood and stretched. The sight of him in nothing but tight black leather trousers left Rowan breathless.

"I believe I promised you a spanking," Lorcan said. "And you'll learn that I always keep my word. As we've just eaten, I won't put you over my knee or the spanking bench. You can lean over the bed." He strolled over to his luggage. "I'm sure there are plenty of paddles and floggers provided here, but I packed my favorite crop so, until I've explored the facilities a bit more, the crop it will be. Followed by my hand, because there's nothing better than the personal touch, don't you agree?"

Rowan had no idea what to say. His pulse was racing and it was all he could do to maintain a semblance of calmness.

Lorcan retrieved the crop. He snapped it against the side of his leg, the sound loud in the quiet of the room. Rowan fancied he could hear his own heart beating, it was pounding so hard.

"Get into position, please." Lorcan flexed his fingers and twirled the crop like a majorette with a baton.

There was no way he could fail to notice Rowan's burgeoning erection as he rose from his knees then walked across to the bed. Lorcan gave him a knowing glance.

"Come again without permission and I can promise you won't enjoy your punishment."

A glass dish on the dresser held a variety of cock rings, which Lorcan seemed to find fascinating. He debated over his choice.

"Leather, metal or rubber? Hmm. Leather will look good against your skin, but steel is more constricting. Steel it is. Turn around, Rowan, and spread your legs so I can put this on you."

Rowan straightened from his position bending over the bed then turned around. As Lorcan fastened the thick metal ring around the base of his balls, Rowan squeezed his eyes shut, praying to every god he could remember to stop him from coming. It was a relief to be able to bend over the bed again so Lorcan couldn't see his face, which Rowan guessed was the color of a post box. A strand of hair flopped over his eyes, tickling his nose.

"Six with the crop. Six with my hand," Lorcan stated.

Rowan locked his elbows but when the first blow came he still lost his balance. Lorcan gave him time to recover before adding five more searing lines of heat across Rowan's arse.

"Beautiful. Your skin takes color well."

A sarcastic retort rose to Rowan's lips but he kept silent. He was grateful for the cock ring when Lorcan stroked his heated cheeks, pushing a finger down Rowan's crack to brush his hole. Rowan shuddered and sank his teeth into his lower lip.

Lorcan didn't drag out the spanking. He delivered six smacks of equal force, three to each cheek. Tears welled in Rowan's eyes, not because of the pain but because the spanking was over. He bit back a sob.

"Lie face down on the bed, Rowan."

Rowan listened as Lorcan went to the bathroom but returned almost immediately.

"I spotted this balm when I took my shower earlier. I want you to lie still while I apply it. I don't want you to bruise."

The ointment was cool and soothing, but it was Lorcan's gentle touch that made the most difference. Rowan rested his head on his folded arms and focused on registering every contact. Lorcan's hands weren't as smooth as he might have expected — there were calluses on the pads below his fingers, making Rowan wonder how Lorcan had acquired them. The pressure on Rowan's arse was delicious, a sensuous mix of pain and pleasure. He twisted his head, trying to see how well the marks stood out, but couldn't get a good view of his backside.

"Neat red stripes topped with a perfect, pink blush," Lorcan said, apparently reading his mind. "Now, keep still."

He smoothed more gel onto Rowan's heated skin and Rowan fancied that he was enjoying the experience just as much as Rowan. His touch lingered longer than necessary and his fingers strayed toward Rowan's hole as if drawn there by magnetic attraction.

"I want you to lie here while this stuff soaks in. I'm going to go and have a chat with Luke Redding. When you're ready, you can unpack my bags and put everything away. No touching the cock ring. If I even suspect that your hands have been anywhere near your dick, you'll find out what an utter bastard I can be."

"Yes, Sir." Rowan wondered what the world record for staying hard was. He had to have a chance at beating it. He giggled at the thought of a man from the *Guinness Book of Records* following him around with a stopwatch. Instead of making his erection flag, Lorcan's threats just made him harder. To Rowan's disappointment, Lorcan pulled on a T-shirt. He perched on the edge of the bed while he put on socks and boots then gave Rowan's backside a gentle pat before he left the room.

Rowan lay still for a few minutes but he wasn't sure how long Lorcan was going to be and wanted to have everything stowed away before he returned so he soon got up. He heaved the first bag onto the bed then unzipped it. He lifted out the neat piles of clothes before sorting them into stacks of trousers, pullovers, T-shirts et cetera. Putting everything into the available storage, in drawers and in the wardrobe, was a pleasure. Lorcan's clothing wasn't fancy, quite utilitarian in fact, but was of excellent quality. Rowan enjoyed the textures of cotton, silk and leather sliding over his skin. It crossed his mind that doing chores with no clothes on was a strange situation to be in, but he guessed it was something that he was going to have to get used to. In the scheme of world problems, it was a minor one.

Lorcan's second bag held an assortment of items, including sportswear, toiletries and a soft leather bag which contained a set of worn leather cuffs and a stiff collar as well as a set of what Rowan guessed were nipple clamps and a spiked, metal cock ring, the sight of which made his cock ache. He zipped the bag closed then placed it in the bottom drawer of the dresser.

It didn't take him long to deal with the rest of Lorcan's belongings. He placed his laptop and satchel on the desk without opening them. The cases he placed outside the door so that they could be put in storage for the duration of Lorcan's stay — something he would deal with later. With the unpacking done, Rowan took the opportunity to clean the bathroom and make the bed. He gave the room a final check over, satisfied that everything was in order. It had been just over an hour since Lorcan left the room and Rowan missed him. He settled onto his knees facing the door and prepared to wait.

It had been an intense day so far. Rowan replayed the highlights in his head. Waiting in the lobby for Lorcan to arrive that morning had been terrifying. He had worried that Lorcan would take one look at him and decide that he wasn't suitable to serve. Instead, Lorcan had lived up to Rowan's highest expectations of how a good Dominant should behave. He wondered what could have happened in Lorcan's life to give him nightmares. Rowan touched his cheek, remembering how Lorcan had thrashed around in the bed. His face didn't hurt anymore and when he'd checked his reflection in the bathroom mirror the slight red mark that remained was hardly visible. Perhaps it had been the journey and Lorcan's exhaustion that had unsettled him, but Rowan had the impression from what Lorcan had said that the nightmares were a regular occurrence.

Rowan wouldn't dare ask for more information but he hoped that, perhaps, Lorcan might tell him, in time.

The spanking Lorcan had delivered would populate Rowan's dreams for some time to come. He had enjoyed the pain more than he'd expected to and hadn't wanted the experience to end. He smiled, guessing that spankings might feature regularly in his life for the next few weeks. That didn't worry him, but he was a little concerned about Lorcan's threat of chastity. It wasn't something he had experienced or felt that he was likely to enjoy, but then it wouldn't be for his pleasure but Lorcan's. It was on the list of things he had agreed to in his contract, as were several other things he had no experience of. He had only ruled out those practices that gave him cold chills of horror. Those he didn't want to think about.

He imagined how it might feel for Lorcan to fuck him. The man was well endowed and Rowan loved to be filled. Though it wasn't part of his contract he hoped that Lorcan might want to negotiate on that point. Rowan shifted on his knees, resisting the temptation to stroke his aching shaft. The cock ring seemed to be growing more restrictive and Rowan sighed, knowing that the situation wasn't likely to change anytime soon. He was so lost in his own thoughts that the door opened without him noticing.

"It seems I'll have to work harder to keep your attention, Rowan."

Rowan gasped. "I'm sorry, Sir. I confess, I was daydreaming."

"About me, I hope."

"Yes, Sir," Rowan whispered.

"And that's something we'll have to discuss in more detail," Lorcan said. "But for now, I promised Mr.

Redding I would send you down to speak to him. He wants to see for himself that I haven't damaged you too badly."

"But it was an accident, Sir," Rowan protested.

"Still, it's his prerogative to be concerned. He's responsible for your safety." Lorcan tousled his hair. "Thank you for unpacking everything, by the way."

"It was my pleasure, Sir."

"Put your underwear on before you go downstairs."

Rowan scrambled to pull on the skimpy briefs. "I'll be as quick as I can, Sir."

"I'm sure you will. When you get back, you can give me a tour of the house. I'm looking forward to seeing everything The Retreat has to offer."

Lorcan held the door open for him, which brought heat to Rowan's cheeks. He ducked his head as he passed, suddenly shy. Not looking where he was going meant that he banged his elbow on the door frame.

"Ow." He rubbed at the sore spot.

Lorcan sighed. "Luke is going to think that I spend the entire time beating you."

"I've always been clumsy, Sir," Rowan said. "If I manage to get through an entire day without gaining a new bruise or scrape, it's something of a miracle."

Lorcan shook his head. "Well, get down there before you do any more damage and Luke throws me out on my ear. And be careful. I'd prefer any bruises on your body to have come from me, by mutual agreement and for both our pleasure."

He closed the door and Rowan trotted down the stairs to his boss's office. The door was closed so he gave it a light tap.

"Come in, Rowan."

Rowan went into the office, pulling the door shut behind him. Luke Redding was seated behind his expansive desk, his expression serious. He pushed his chair back then stood, before circling the desk to stand in front of Rowan.

"How's your face? Mr. Wilder told me what happened, but I want to hear it from you."

"It's nothing, sir, and it *was* an accident. Mr. Wilder was sleeping but he was having a bad dream. I tried to wake him and as he came to, he swung his arm up as if he was defending himself from something. He caught my face with the back of his hand. He apologized, even though there was no need. He didn't know what he was doing when it happened."

"Thank you for explaining, Rowan. I hope you don't think I'm overreacting, but your safety is very important to me. I'm content that this happened as you've explained. You're happy to continue in your role as Mr. Wilder's submissive?"

"Oh! Yes, sir. All the signs are that he's a wonderful Dom. I feel safe with him, I can assure you."

"He tells me he's been pushing you quite hard already. You remember the traffic light system? If you need him to slow down at any time, just say 'amber'. You won't lose his respect, or mine, if you need to take a break."

"I understand, Mr. Redding."

"Then you may go. I'm here if you need me."

Rowan nodded and made a hasty exit. Luke Redding made him nervous with his intensity. He scampered back upstairs to the Blue Room, excited about what the rest of the day might bring.

Chapter Six

Lorcan sat back in his well-padded chair and contemplated his situation. He had just eaten three courses of the most amazing food, served by a young man in kitchen whites who was deferential without being obsequious. Now, he sipped wine from a lead crystal goblet and if he had been more of a wine snob he would have come up with an array of superlatives to describe the flavors bursting over his tongue. He had left the choice of wine to the chef, letting him know that he preferred lighter vintages but that otherwise he was happy to submit to his guidance. It had been the right decision because the Merlot had perfectly complemented the food. The dining table was set in a room that Rowan, during a tour of the house, had called the snug. Lorcan thought it was an apt name for the cozy, wood-paneled space. One wall was lined with bookcases while on another a mullioned window gave a view of the extensive grounds. In the distance, the forest canopy shifted in the wind, forming a protective boundary around the property.

"The meal was absolutely delicious," Lorcan said, addressing Rowan who knelt on the floor next to him. "I'd like to give my compliments to the chef. Would you fetch him for me please, Rowan? His name's Tor, isn't it?"

"Yes, Sir." Rowan rose from his knees. It was something he seemed able to do without his usual clumsiness. He left the room and for a while the only sound came from classical music playing over a concealed speaker system. Lorcan allowed his eyes to drift shut. He hadn't had enough sleep earlier in the day and now jet lag was sinking its soporific talons into his body. If he was tired enough then perhaps his sleep wouldn't be interrupted by more nightmares. He heard the slightest creak from the door and opened his eyes. Rowan came in first, followed by a tall blond dressed in a chef's uniform. He had a similar military bearing to Luke Redding, walking almost as if he were on parade.

Lorcan got to his feet, moving around the table to approach Tor. He held out his hand. "I apologize for pulling you away from your work, Tor, but I had to let you know how much I enjoyed that meal. My stay here is going to be a considerable pleasure if the dishes you serve are always of this standard."

Tor shook his hand, his grip firm but not crushing, as if he had nothing to prove.

"It's my pleasure, Mr. Wilder. I love my job. However, I can't take all the credit—I have two very able assistants who make my life easy."

"I'd ask you to join me for a drink, but I'm afraid I'm not very good company tonight. Jet lag is kicking my butt. But another night, perhaps?"

"If it gives me an excuse to get out of the washing up, it will be my pleasure." Tor's eyes twinkled. Lorcan couldn't picture him up to his elbows in soapy water but he seemed like the kind of man who would lead by example. It wouldn't surprise Lorcan if he did take his turn with more menial tasks.

"Is there anything I can do to make things easier for you in the kitchen?" Lorcan asked.

"Timing is the main thing," Tor replied. "It would be helpful if Rowan could give me a list of mealtimes each evening for the next day, approximate is fine, and let me know where you'd prefer to be served. I can give him the menus for the day if you'd like to see them, that's if you're happy for me to pick them."

"I'm sure I can accommodate you with the timing plans. I have no intention of interfering in your menu choices. There are very few things I won't eat and you have a list of those. As Rowan will usually be dining with me, I assume you're aware of his dislikes too?"

"Yes, I have details for all the staff, so that won't be a problem and thank you for trusting me with menu selection. It's one of the things I most enjoy about my job. But of course, if there's anything you are particularly craving then let me know."

"I'll no doubt get a hankering for a hotdog at some point." Lorcan laughed. "But don't let me succumb. I'm not here to eat junk food."

"Then I'll leave you to get a good night's rest. Send Rowan to the kitchen later. I'll still be there." Tor departed and Lorcan remained standing. He ruffled Rowan's hair.

"Time for bed, I think."

"Yes, Sir."

"I expect you're tired too, Rowan. It's been a long day for you."

"I'm fine, Sir. Though the food has made me a little drowsy, I have to admit."

Lorcan led the way back upstairs to the Blue Room, which he now considered *his* room. Rowan turned down the bed.

"Would you like me to run you a bath, Sir?"

"That sounds like a great idea," Lorcan said. "I don't often have the time for more than a quick shower."

Rowan went into the bathroom and Lorcan listened to the rush of running water. A light citrus scent wafted through the door on a cloud of steam. He stripped out of his clothes, dumping everything on the bed apart from his boots. Rowan would know what to do with it all. He padded through to the en suite, where Rowan knelt next to the tub, swishing his hand through the water to test its temperature.

"I think this is perfect, Sir."

Lorcan stepped into the water, sinking down until it covered him to the neck. The heat soaked into his muscles. He slid lower until he was submerged, then surfaced shaking droplets from his hair.

"It would be more perfect, if you were in here with me, Rowan."

"Oh…"

Rowan had a deer-caught-in-the-headlights expression, but removed his trousers—all he was wearing—without hesitation. The bath was plenty big enough for two people. He stepped in, straddling Lorcan's legs, facing him. He went to his knees and his cock bobbed prettily in the water. Lorcan took it in hand, giving it a couple of gentle tugs.

"Tomorrow, I'm going to lock this up." He petted the golden curls that bedded Rowan's shaft. "And I think these have to go."

Rowan's eyes widened but he didn't say anything. In Lorcan's hand, Rowan's cock hardened. He was still wearing the cock ring and Lorcan realized that he should have changed the metal one for something better suited to immersion. He let himself off because he was so tired, but made a mental note to pay better attention to Rowan's needs.

Rowan took a natural sponge from the side of the bath and lathered it with soap. He rubbed the sponge over Lorcan's body. Lorcan knew he should have reprimanded him for taking the initiative without being asked, but the sensation was too good to complain about. He closed his eyes and allowed Rowan to wash him. His cock hardened and stayed that way until, ten minutes later, he stepped out of the bath into a warm towel Rowan held open for him. He pulled Rowan closer, enfolding him within the towel.

"You need to get dry, too."

Rowan wriggled from his grip, dropping to his knees. He looked up, licking his lips.

"May I, Sir?"

Lorcan braced himself with one hand on the sink before nodding his assent.

"Wait. You're sure? We haven't discussed this."

"It *is* in the contract, Sir," Rowan reminded him. His lips closed around Lorcan's shaft, applying perfect pressure. He took Lorcan's dick deep into his throat and, though he gagged a little at the first attempt, the second time was seamless. He sucked hard and Lorcan wound the fingers of his free hand into Rowan's damp hair, holding him in place. He took control, fucking Rowan's willing mouth. It took only seconds to reach orgasm. Lorcan shuddered as he came, his release providing a symbolic break between his old life and the new. Sated, he let his cock slip from Rowan's mouth. Rowan's angelic smile let him know that he hadn't been too rough.

"You've given me plenty of material for my dreams tonight, Rowan. Once you are dry and dressed, you may go. Remove the cock ring. Just call in at the kitchen and let Tor know that I'll take breakfast at nine, a light lunch at one and dinner at eight, all in the same room we used this evening."

Rowan pulled on the trousers he had worn to dinner.

"If you're sure there's nothing more I can do for you this evening, Sir, sleep well. What time would you like me to wake you in the morning?"

"You can present yourself at seven to accept your morning discipline." Lorcan didn't expand. It would be good for Rowan to wonder what that meant overnight. "Wear something inspiring."

"Yes, Sir." Rowan's cheeks were flushed with color, his eyes bright. The temptation to throw him down on the bed and fuck him hard was strong. Lorcan didn't think Rowan would be averse to the idea, but a conversation would be needed before that step was taken. They had only been together for a day, though it seemed to Lorcan that Rowan had been made just for him, and an easy conquest was not as much fun as a lengthier campaign.

Rowan left, closing the door quietly behind him and Lorcan immediately regretted sending him away. He determined that it would be the last night he spent alone. Chaining Rowan to his bed had all kinds of interesting possibilities.

* * * *

Rowan didn't sleep well. He set his alarm for six to be sure that he had plenty of time to get ready to be at Lorcan's room on the dot of seven. He woke long before it went off, having only dozed intermittently between dreams that left him panting and overheated. He gave up on rest and instead took his time in the shower. He made use of the enema kit in the bathroom cupboard, an experience he tolerated rather than enjoyed. Clean from top to bottom, inside and out, he debated what to wear. Lorcan had asked for something inspiring, but Rowan wasn't sure what that meant. His outfit the previous day had been skimpy in the extreme so it was a safe bet that Lorcan wouldn't want him covered up.

He dug through the dresser drawers, pulling out a selection of the underwear that had been left there for him. The range was extensive and there was little he would have chosen for himself unless, of course, he had been accompanied on a shopping expedition by Ed, who seemed to think that less was more where undergarments were concerned. Rowan grinned when he thought about his friend. It had been too late to ring him the previous night and besides, Rowan wasn't quite ready to share his experiences yet. He wanted to be selfish and keep Lorcan to himself for a while. Thinking about Ed made him search through the drawers a little bit further. His unpacking had been rushed and he had shoved his own clothes to the back, resolving to sort everything out when he had a few hours to himself. He soon found the pair of black latex shorts he had bought for his interview but never worn. He eyed them with suspicion, not sure whether he had the courage to wear them.

"You wandered around all day yesterday with your arse on display, so what's the problem?" Giving himself a talking-to helped a bit. He took the shorts into the bathroom where he had spotted a container of talcum powder. He applied a liberal sprinkling before shimmying into the shorts. They had some stretch, which was fortunate because there wasn't a millimeter of spare room inside them. No matter how Rowan adjusted himself, the ridge of his cock was clearly visible and the latex seemed to sink between his arse cheeks. The shorts rode so low on his hips that he knew if he got an erection there was no doubt that his dick would poke over the top. He sighed. Lorcan would either like that or punish him for it. Rowan wasn't sure which option he preferred.

He checked the time. He still had twenty minutes before he needed to be at Lorcan's room. He debated whether or not to use the time to jack off and give himself some breathing space before he had to worry about an erection, but the thought of getting out of the shorts and then back into them again put him off. He took the time to send a quick text to Ed, promising to call him as soon as he could, though he wasn't sure when that might be. He didn't expect a reply but his phone immediately chimed with the alert for an incoming message. Ed had sent him a picture and he had to wait a few seconds for it to download. When it finally opened, Rowan snorted his laughter. The picture was of a man on his hands and knees wearing full puppy play regalia and a pair of shorts not unlike those Rowan had on. The only difference was the shorts had a split down the back and the man had a butt plug inserted that looked like a tail. Ed's internet research on Rowan's behalf was definitely expanding his view of the world.

Rowan left his room in plenty of time and presented himself at Lorcan's door five minutes before he was due. He knocked, hoping that Lorcan was already awake. The door swung open almost as if Lorcan had been waiting behind it. He was dressed in snug-fitting exercise clothes and trainers.

"Good morning, Rowan. Your clothing choices are very much to my satisfaction." He held the door open. "Come in. Bend over the bed."

Rowan did as he was ordered, pulse pounding. Lorcan stood close behind him, his hands on Rowan's hips.

"For the duration of my stay, this will be your routine in the morning. It's important to re-establish our roles for the day, and that means discipline. I'll deliver three swats with an instrument of my choice. You will count and thank me for each stroke."

"Yes, Sir." Rowan was proud his voice didn't shake.

Lorcan slipped his hands into each side of Rowan's shorts, pushing them down to his thighs.

"It's a shame you're not plugged. It would make this experience so much more enjoyable for both of us. It's something that I will ensure is corrected tomorrow."

Rowan gulped. He didn't trust himself to respond.

"You seemed to enjoy the crop yesterday so that's what I'm going to use this morning," Lorcan stated. He gave Rowan's arse a pat.

Rowan took a deep breath and shifted his feet a little further apart to get better balance. The anticipation of pain made him hard and he had no cock ring to help him control himself. He sank his teeth into his lower lip, worrying the tender flesh. When the first stroke of the crop landed across his backside, he yelped.

"One. Thank you, Sir."

The second stroke was harder and Rowan didn't feel that grateful when he said thank you. Lorcan had delivered one swat per cheek. The third was horizontal, intersecting both previous lines of fire that burned Rowan's flesh.

"Three. Thank you, Sir." He held his position despite the desperate urge to rub his rear.

"You took those beautifully," Lorcan said. "Stay as you are while I fetch the balm."

Rowan had no intention of moving. He took a few deep breaths. Glancing down, he gave his rock-hard cock a baleful glare until his attention was drawn to Lorcan smoothing cold gel over his burning cheeks.

"I can see you enjoyed our start to the day," Lorcan said.

"To be honest, Sir, I don't know whether to cry or ask for more," Rowan admitted.

Lorcan, his fingers still slick with cooling balm, cupped Rowan's balls. He massaged them with deft strokes.

"If you can come just from this touch, you have my permission."

"Won't be a problem, Sir." Rowan could barely get the words out. His entire body shuddered as he came, spurting onto the bed clothes. His knees gave way, but Lorcan held him up, pulling him into an embrace.

"I slept well last night thanks to you. I feel great and spanking you is an excellent warm up for a workout."

"I'm glad to be of assistance. My arse is at your service."

"It is and you have my gratitude." He kneaded Rowan's backside. "I shouldn't be more than an hour, assuming I can still find the gym. You have things to do here?"

"I can show you the way first, if you'd like me to, Sir?"

"I'll manage. Then by the time I'm done and showered, we can go to breakfast." Lorcan stepped towards the door. "You okay?"

Rowan locked his knees. "Yes, Sir. Enjoy your workout."

As soon as Lorcan had gone, Rowan gave his sore behind a rub, moaning at the pleasure pain of the ache. He pulled his shorts up, wishing he'd opted for silk or soft cotton instead of latex, but hindsight was a wonderful thing. He'd just have to hope they didn't chafe too much while he got on with his chores. He collected all the cleaning supplies that he needed from storage, catching sight of Luke in the hallway as he crossed the gallery. Luke nodded in his direction then continued toward his office.

Rowan tackled the bathroom first, though Lorcan wasn't untidy, cleaning the sink, toilet and shower until they gleamed. The bath got a good scrub as well. Rowan collected up the towels and put them in a pile next to the bedroom door. He stripped the bed, adding the linens to the heap for the laundry, then went to collect fresh stock. Posting all the things for washing down the laundry chute was fun and he breathed deeply when he opened the door of the linen cupboard because the smell of scented cotton made him happy. Back in Lorcan's room, he put clean towels on the bathroom radiator to warm through then made up the bed, smoothing the covers and plumping the pillows.

Finally, he gave the furniture a quick dust and tidied anything that was out of place. He opened the window a crack to let in some fresh air then stowed all the cleaning gear away in its cupboard. Satisfied that everything was as it should be, Rowan settled on his knees opposite the door and waited for Lorcan to return. The position calmed him. He couldn't make mistakes or bump into things when he was kneeling.

Lorcan whipped off his shirt the instant he came through the door. His face and chest were pink, glistening with a fine sheen of sweat. Rowan's mouth went dry. He found a spot on the carpet to focus on but couldn't resist peeking through his lashes. Lorcan's self-satisfied smirk told him he'd been spotted.

"Enjoying the view, Rowan?"

"Yes, Sir." Rowan decided honesty was the best policy because it meant he had an excuse to stare at Lorcan's sculpted chest.

Lorcan kicked off his trainers, toed off his socks then dropped his tracksuit bottoms. He was left wearing a snowy white jock and a smile. He chuckled then headed for the bathroom giving Rowan a perfect view of his impressive arse.

"Holy fuck," Rowan muttered under his breath. He didn't swear often but Lorcan's body was worthy of a few well-chosen expletives.

"Get in here, Rowan!" Lorcan sounded more amused than impatient.

Rowan scrambled to his feet. By the time he got into the bathroom, Lorcan was beneath the shower, soaping his body.

He's doing it deliberately, I know he is. Rowan watched, wide-eyed, as Lorcan washed his cock and balls. *He's torturing me.* Rowan's shorts were far too small to contain his burgeoning erection. He tried to adjust himself, but the latex was tight and his cock persistent. He gave up with a pained sigh, resigned to a morning of discomfort and humiliation. Lorcan would love his predicament, that was certain. Rowan grabbed the bath towel and held it out, partly to shield himself but also so that Lorcan could step out of the shower into its warmth. Of course, when the towel was wrapped around Lorcan's hips, Rowan lost its protection. Lorcan's gaze went immediately to Rowan's groin.

"This morning, I'm going to do something about that problem you have there," he said. "But first, I need to fortify myself with one of Tor's no doubt delicious breakfasts. Why don't you go on downstairs, Rowan? Check that everything is ready. You can join me at the table this morning, so make sure there's a place setting for you."

Rowan escaped with relief, though, as he descended the stairs, he prayed that Tor would not be in the snug. Rowan found Tor a little intimidating and, though he knew the chef wouldn't bat an eyelid at Rowan's condition, he also knew the information would be filed away and add to the impression he was making. He wouldn't be buying a Lottery ticket anytime soon because sure enough, when he reached the snug, Tor was laying out a basket of fresh bread. The aroma was enticing and Rowan almost forgot the state he was in until Tor pinned him with a knowing stare, eyebrows raised.

"Good morning, Chef." Heat bloomed in Rowan's cheeks.

"It is indeed, boy." Tor didn't smile but his lips twitched.

"Mr. Wilder will be down shortly. He wants me to sit at the table with him." Rowan noted that there was only one place setting laid out.

"Then you'd better come to the kitchen with me," Tor said. "I'll give you some more crockery and cutlery."

The walk to the kitchen and back didn't help Rowan's predicament. The friction against his rigid shaft was torment. It was a miracle he made it back to the snug without dropping anything. He'd just finished setting everything out when Lorcan arrived. Rowan waited for him to take his seat before taking his own chair.

"Help yourself, Rowan. No need to stand on ceremony, but I suggest you have a light meal. This morning will be…quite demanding."

Rowan sighed. If Lorcan had anything to do with it Rowan would be hard for the rest of his life. Just the stern tone of his voice sent lightning bolts of arousal to Rowan's cock. He wished Lorcan would be a bit more forthcoming about his plans for the morning but of course he said nothing, choosing instead to make small talk about the food, the delicious coffee and even the weather. It was the longest meal Rowan had ever sat through. When Lorcan poured himself another cup of coffee, Rowan wanted to throw it at him.

"You seem a little agitated," Lorcan said, stirring a few grains of sugar into his drink. "You serve at my pleasure, Rowan. Suffice to say I think you'll enjoy this morning's activities." He pointed at the floor. "Next to me please."

It was a relief to get to his knees, even though the floor was hard, because it meant that he no longer had to make eye contact. Rowan forced himself to relax and take deep breaths. Lorcan cupped the nape of his neck with a warm hand.

"I know you're going to do well for me this morning. Just do your best. I don't expect anything more." He sipped his coffee. "It's time we paid our first visit to the dungeon."

Rowan shivered, the hair rising on his forearms. He determined to try his best to be what Lorcan needed. It was no hardship to please him. Lorcan stroked his neck, calming him as he might a skittish colt. Rowan pressed into his touch, seeking the reassurance it provided.

"Good boy. Everything is going to be fine. I'm here and I'll take care of you."

Rowan had no doubt it was true. He may have only known him for a short time but Rowan trusted Lorcan with every fiber of his being. His errant cock twitched, eager to get started. Rowan wished his mind could be as confident as his body apparently was that he would find the morning's events pleasurable.

Chapter Seven

Rowan took the lead down the steps to the dungeon, his bare feet silent on the flagstones. Lorcan kept a close eye on him, ready to catch him if he stumbled, because he seemed a little shaky. Lorcan wanted him to be excited about the morning ahead, even nervous, but not scared. Definitely not scared. The lighting was dim enough that equipment loomed out of the darkness. Lorcan ignored the main room and headed straight for one of the doors set into the wall. When Rowan had given him a tour of the facilities Lorcan had known immediately that this cell would suit his purposes. It contained a vertical iron frame, rectangular in shape and set on a platform raising it about a foot off the floor. He reckoned it was about seven feet high, five feet wide and was kept stable by posts anchoring it to the ceiling. Chains were riveted to each corner of the frame, heavy iron manacles at their ends. The frame was perfect for displaying a man whilst rendering him completely helpless. Lorcan knew that Rowan would look stunning chained and spread for his pleasure.

Once they were both inside the small room, Lorcan closed the door. It shut with a clang, making Rowan jump.

"I want you naked."

Lorcan watched as Rowan peeled off his latex shorts. He assumed a display position with his hands behind his head, fingers interlaced and legs apart. His cock bounced as he moved, still hard. Anticipation of what might happen had not worried him enough to deflate his erection. Lorcan stripped off his shirt, wanting to feel the cool air against his skin. He could sense Rowan's gaze on him, watching his every move.

"Step up onto the platform, Rowan, and spread your legs."

It was a high step up and Rowan wobbled as he took it. Lorcan steadied him with a hand on his ass, noting that it was still flushed with color just as it should be.

"That's it, facing me."

The bar at the base of the frame was wide enough for Rowan to stand on without hurting his feet. Lorcan locked a manacle around each slender ankle. Rowan seemed fascinated as the metal clicked shut, tight against his skin.

"If you struggle, the metal will hurt you, so keep still," Lorcan said. "Luke told me that you're familiar with the traffic light system. If you want me to slow down at any time, what do you say?"

"Amber, Sir," Rowan said, a slight tremble in his voice.

"And red to stop. Okay?"

Rowan nodded, eyes wide.

"Present your wrist to the cuff," Lorcan ordered.

Rowan reached for the corner of the frame and Lorcan enclosed his wrist in metal. He had to stand on the platform in order to reach. He repeated the process with Rowan's other wrist, leaving him displayed in an X shape.

"Stunning." He ran his hands down Rowan's flanks to his thighs. "You present a very pretty picture, Rowan. Now, I'm going to fetch a few things. I'll only be a couple of minutes and I won't leave the dungeon. You'll be able to hear me moving around. I won't be far away and I promise I will never leave you alone when you're in bondage."

Lorcan left the cell door wide open while he went to fetch the things he needed from the storage cupboards in the main room. There were so many wonderful toys to choose from but he knew what he wanted. He stopped at the deep butler's sink to fill a metal bowl with water then carried it and his collection of other items back to the cell.

Rowan's lips were parted and his breaths were coming fast. He eyed Lorcan's burdens with interest. Lorcan put everything onto a low bench before circling behind the frame. Rowan's ass muscles clenched under his scrutiny and Lorcan couldn't resist touching. He stroked the curve of Rowan's backside then slid a finger between his cheeks to brush his hole. Rowan gave the sweetest whimper and jerked in his chains.

"Remember what I said. Keep still, or you will have bruises on your wrists and ankles. Or maybe you'd like that? A little reminder of our morning together. Marks you can see, not like the ones I put on your ass."

Lorcan walked around the platform to stand in front of Rowan. He took hold of his dick, giving it a couple of firm tugs, before running his fingertips through the golden curls at its base.

"I told you these would have to go, didn't I?" He fetched the bowl of water and placed it on the platform next to one of Rowan's feet. He set a razor and a stick of shaving soap next to it. "First, a trim." A sharp pair of manicure scissors made quick work of Rowan's curls. Lorcan cropped the hair as short as he could before wetting the shaving stick and rubbing it to create a lather. He spread the creamy white froth around Rowan's groin then began to shave him, being careful to follow the line of hair so as not to cause too much irritation. Each time he moved Rowan's cock out of the way he was rewarded by faint mewling sounds and the rattle of chains. Rowan's balls were hot and weighty in Lorcan's hand. He shaved with care before rinsing all traces of the cream away.

"Just think how sensitive you're going to be now." Lorcan cleared away the shaving equipment then applied a layer of moisturizer to Rowan's newly bared skin. He stood back to admire his work then gave the tip of Rowan's cock a sharp flick. "You want to come, Rowan?"

"Please! Yes! I mean... If it pleases you, Sir."

Lorcan contemplated the idea of making Rowan suffer a bit longer, but it suited his purpose to have him come. He undid his belt and slipped it from its loops. The end would make an excellent makeshift flogger. He slapped Rowan's cock with the leather, once, twice... Then gave his balls a light smack. Rowan's hips jerked and he came in a gush, his scream no doubt a combination of pain and the pleasure of release.

"Oh God!" Rowan tugged on his chains.

Lorcan smiled. Rowan skin was flushed. Sweat-dampened tendrils of hair stuck to his forehead. His eyes were wild, his line of sight darting here and there. Lorcan balanced the weight of Rowan's softening cock in his palm.

"So sensitive. But now it's time to lock this away. I'm very possessive, Rowan, and I want to keep it all for myself. Nobody else gets to touch it, not even you."

He went over to the bench to collect the chastity device he had selected. To begin with, he had wanted to use something heavy, fashioned from stainless steel, but this option was more practical as Rowan would be wearing it for long periods of time. He held the device up for Rowan to see.

"The cock ring component of this device has nice rounded edges so you won't feel any pinching. It has an ingenious locking system, which doesn't require a padlock, just a key to engage the mechanism." Lorcan fitted the device, taking his time to make sure it was in the correct position. "It's made of some clever material that molds to your shape as it's heated, so the more you wear it the more comfortable it becomes. There are no metal parts so you can even wear it through an airport scanner and, unless you're wearing something extremely tight, it won't be visible under your clothes. Only you and I will know you're in chastity." There were air holes on the front of the cage for ventilation and a slit to allow Rowan to relieve himself. Once it was in place and locked, Lorcan was pleased with the way that it looked. The acrylic was clear rather than opaque and there was something infinitely satisfying about seeing Rowan's tender flesh confined in the restrictive tube.

"How does it feel? Is anything pinching?" Rowan wouldn't be able to fully describe how it felt until he was able to move around, but he'd know if any part of it was causing him pain.

"No, Sir… It feels strange, but nothing hurts." Rowan bent his head, trying to get a look.

"You'll have time to examine it soon enough," Lorcan said. "But in the meantime, I have one last treat for you." He fetched lube and a bulbous plug from the bench. "This should keep your mind occupied." He slathered the plug with a thick coating of gel before circling the platform once more to stand behind Rowan. He parted Rowan's cheeks with one hand and pushed the blunt end of the plug against his hole with the other. "Relax. This is what I want, so you'll let it in." He applied some pressure, breaching Rowan's guardian muscle. Rowan let out a rush of breath and moaned.

"It's big, Sir."

"Nothing you can't handle." Lorcan pushed steadily, watching with satisfaction as Rowan's body absorbed the widest part of the toy. The rest slid home with ease, leaving just the black base visible. Lorcan gave it a jiggle, eliciting a loud groan from his victim. "I'll have to find a harness for you to help keep this inside, though the shape and size should mean that it won't slip out easily." He gave Rowan's ass a pat.

"Thank you, Sir. That's very considerate of you."

"Brats get spankings," Lorcan threatened, responding to Rowan sarcastic tone. He moved to lean against the door, taking in the picture he had created. His naked sub chained and plugged, his dick caged. The vision was inspiring.

"How are your arms? Any loss of feeling in your fingers?"

"No, Sir." Rowan wiggled them in demonstration.

"Good." Lorcan unzipped his fly and took a firm hold of his cock. It would be preferable to have Rowan's lips wrapped around his swollen member, but his sadistic streak wanted to torment Rowan a bit further. He jacked himself with leisurely strokes, humming his pleasure, keeping eye contact with Rowan. He was glad of the support the door provided because when he came, his entire body shuddered through the release. It took him a while to compose himself but when he was steady on his feet again he left the cell to clean up. When he returned, he pulled on his jeans and T-shirt and shoved bare feet into his boots. He unchained Rowan's ankles first then reached for a wrist cuff.

"This may hurt some." He lowered Rowan's arm, supporting it until it could rest against Rowan's side.

"It burns a bit, Sir."

Lorcan massaged his shoulder before releasing his other wrist. He kneaded the tense muscles until Rowan sighed and leaned into him.

"It's been quite a morning, hasn't it?" Lorcan petted Rowan's hair. "I think it might be my turn to run you a bath, then there should be time for a quick nap before lunch."

Against Lorcan's neck, Rowan murmured something unintelligible.

"I'll take that as agreement," Lorcan said, smiling. "I'm proud of you, Rowan, you've done so well. You may only be mine for a few short weeks, but I'm glad you are. Be warned, it's very possible I may not be able to let you go."

* * * *

Rowan awoke in Lorcan's bed, the fifth morning in a row that he had done so. The first week of Lorcan's stay had passed in a flash and sometimes, in the new light of dawn, Rowan wondered if he had dreamed it all. A slight snore from next to him brought him back to reality. Rowan loved to watch Lorcan sleep. It was the only time the man ever seemed to truly relax — but only after Rowan had coaxed him through his nightmares. He'd discovered that Lorcan responded to being held. Rowan never failed to wake when Lorcan's breathing sped up and his limbs twitched, indicating the start of a bad dream. If he cuddled close and stroked Lorcan's skin he always calmed, and woke with no memory of what had tormented his subconscious.

Rowan never raised the subject of the nightmares. It wasn't his business to pry about what it was that affected Lorcan so deeply. Lorcan was rich, gorgeous and successful — it was hard to imagine what could possibly have happened in his past to leave such deep scars. Rowan slipped his hand beneath the covers to touch the rigid shell encasing his cock. It had been in place since the scene in the dungeon when Lorcan had shaved him. That whole morning had fueled Rowan's fantasies ever since, which didn't do anything for his frustration. He didn't dare ask Lorcan to remove the device even though he would have crawled and begged if he thought that might be the end result, but he knew that Lorcan would take his own sweet time making that decision. He made a point of checking Rowan's cock for sore spots each morning after his discipline and at no time had he ever indicated that he intended to remove the device. It wasn't uncomfortable, but Rowan was hyper aware of its presence. Lorcan's control of his cock also meant he had a certain amount of control over Rowan's mind.

A subtle change in Lorcan's breathing told Rowan that he was awake. He shifted onto his side so that he could look into Lorcan's eyes and be the first thing that Lorcan saw on waking. His dark lashes fluttered then lifted to reveal shards of piercing blue.

"Good morning, beautiful." Lorcan's sleep-roughened voice sent shivers down Rowan's spine.

"Good morning, Sir."

Lorcan snaked a hand around Rowan's body to squeeze his arse. He pushed a finger between Rowan's cheeks, grazing his hole. Rowan shuddered. He ached to be filled. A plug would do, but he hoped and prayed that one day soon Lorcan would want to fuck him.

"I want to talk to you about your contract over breakfast this morning," Lorcan said. "I want to know how you feel about making a couple of changes." Lorcan ran a hand through his hair, leaving it sticking up in spikes. "I'll give you your discipline before I go to the gym then meet you downstairs."

Rowan slipped out of bed to use the bathroom and make sure everything was ready for Lorcan. He laid out his exercise clothes and a chilled bottle of water.

"I'm feeling too lazy to get out of bed yet, so come here and lie across my lap."

Rowan climbed onto the bed and got into position.

"I do love adding color to your skin first thing in the morning," Lorcan said before delivering three hard spanks.

Squirming, Rowan stayed where he was until Lorcan told him he could move. In its plastic prison, his cock tried to harden. The situation only got more frustrating when Lorcan stroked his backside, soothing the ache but doing nothing to relieve his arousal.

"You can dress. Stay dressed for breakfast, too. You are far too distracting with next to nothing on and I want to be focused on our discussion, not your body."

"Yes, Sir." Rowan pulled on his trousers, holding back a smile. Lorcan dictated what he wore so it was entirely his own fault if he got distracted. He left the room, pulling the door closed behind him. From the galleried landing he could see that Luke Redding's door was open and as Rowan descended the stairs, Luke emerged from his office. Rowan paused, lowering his eyes respectfully.

"It's a fine morning, Rowan," Luke said. "How are you?"

"Very good, thank you, Mr. Redding. Mr. Wilder is on his way to the gym and I'm going to make sure everything is ready for breakfast. He says he wants to discuss our contract."

"That's his prerogative," Luke said. "If there's anything you want to talk to me about afterwards, come and find me." He took one of Rowan's hands, lifting his arm to examine his wrist, which was ringed with bruises. "I understand Mr. Wilder has been making good use of the dungeon." He released Rowan's hand.

"Every day," Rowan replied. "It's a great facility."

"So long as everything you do down there is by mutual consent. I know it's your job to serve Mr. Wilder, but that doesn't mean you have to agree to anything you don't want to."

"I know." Rowan examined his bare feet, pale against the plush carpet. "But so far, I've been enjoying myself. A lot." His cheeks heated.

Luke chuckled. "I'm glad to hear it. You get on with what you need to do. Oh, and I meant to ask, could you check with Mr. Wilder if he'll be needing the car today? I have some errands that I'd like Rayne to run for me but I don't want to send him out if he's needed elsewhere."

"He hasn't said he intends to go out today, but I'll check at breakfast then let you know," Rowan said. So far, Lorcan hadn't left The Retreat at all, saying that there was plenty to occupy him inside.

Luke returned to his office and Rowan took a quick detour to his room to check his messages. There was a text from Rory and several from Ed. He scanned through them, giggling at the content, but there was nothing that he needed to respond to straightaway. He took a long, hot shower then changed into fresh pair of jeans and a soft, plain black T-shirt that hugged his frame. He didn't bother with underwear because he thought it likely that he would be changing again later.

The table was laid for breakfast in the snug and Tor was in the process of leaving a pot of coffee as Rowan entered the room. The aroma tickled his nostrils.

"I have some fresh croissants warming this morning, Rowan. Do you think Mr. Wilder would like some?"

Lorcan normally stuck to a very healthy diet but he had confessed to having a secret sweet tooth.

"I'm sure he would," Rowan said. "Especially if there's some of that wonderful home-made jam we had the other day."

"Flattery will get you everywhere," Tor stated. "Especially when it comes to jam. I'll send one of the boys with it when they bring the croissants in because I want to keep them warm."

"Thank you. I have to admit I'll be looking forward to them too." He grinned as Tor gave him a light cuff.

"Naughty boy." He disappeared toward the kitchen, whistling.

"There is a man happy in his work," Rowan murmured. "I know how he feels."

"Talking to yourself, Rowan? Should I be worried?"

Rowan whirled around to find Lorcan lounging against the doorframe, a smug grin on his handsome face. He was wearing tight black jeans and a pale blue open-necked shirt and Rowan knew that if it hadn't been for the cock cage, he would definitely be hard.

"You should be happy, Sir. I was just arranging a treat for you."

Lorcan walked toward him. "I could say that you're the only treat I need, but that would be a lie. I hope this one involves some of Tor's jelly… Sorry, jam. Jelly is Jell-O, right?"

"Yes, Sir. Jelly is the dessert, though we do have bramble jelly, which is a kind of jam."

Lorcan took a seat at the table. "I'm not even gonna ask why that should be. I think you Brits just want to confuse the rest of the world."

"Probably." Rowan hovered near the table, not sure whether he should kneel at Lorcan's side or use the furniture.

"You should consider yourself off the clock for the next hour," Lorcan said. "I want to talk to you man-to-man rather than Master-to-submissive. But before you ask, the chastity device stays."

Rowan didn't feel entirely comfortable as he sat opposite Lorcan at the table, gleaming crockery and glassware a barrier between them. Lorcan poured them both a glass of fresh orange juice and a mug of coffee.

He served himself yogurt and fruit, sprinkling some granola over the top. Rowan sipped his juice, his appetite gone.

"Not hungry?" Lorcan asked.

Rowan shook his head. "Not really. I'm a little nervous."

"It wasn't my intention to make you feel uncomfortable, Rowan," Lorcan said. "I was going to wait until we had eaten, but perhaps it's best to get the serious part of this over with." He sipped his coffee, humming his pleasure.

"Yes please, Sir."

"You can call me Lorcan, sweetheart. I want to discuss your contract, specifically the no sex clause. When I came here, I had no intention of getting too involved. The appeal of this place was having a chance to play without strings. But I didn't consider how you might make me feel. I want to sleep with you, Rowan. I don't mean just to have you in my bed, though I will be satisfied with waking up next to you if this isn't what you want. I'm jealous of the toys I fuck you with. I want to feel you around my cock. I wouldn't suggest it if I didn't think we had an emotional connection, but I've grown to care for you deeply over the last week. You've rekindled parts of me that I thought were long dead."

Rowan blinked, tears welling in his eyes. He hadn't expected such raw honesty.

"Hey, don't get upset." Lorcan shoved his chair back then moved to stand next Rowan. He put his arm around Rowan's shoulders. "We don't have to change a thing, if you don't want to."

"That's not it, Sir... Sorry, Lorcan. I mean, it's what I want too. More than anything." Rowan leaned against Lorcan's warmth. "It's just strange, talking about putting it into a contract when it's something I feel. It should just be between us and have nothing to do with a piece of paper."

"It's for your protection, and believe me when I say I feel *very* protective when it comes to you. How about I just have a quiet word with Luke Redding. He'll want your confirmation but I doubt he'll be surprised."

There was a discrete cough from the direction of the door. Rowan rubbed at his eyes.

"I decided to bring these in myself," Tor said, approaching the table. He left a plate of croissants and a pot of jam on the table then left without saying anything else.

Lorcan squeezed Rowan's shoulder. "This must be my treat. It's turning out to be quite a morning." He resumed his seat, picking up one of the crumbly pastries as he went.

"Would you like to go for a walk this morning?" Rowan asked. "It would be nice to get to know you a bit better. I mean, I know all the things from your file about what you like and dislike, but I don't really *know* you."

"That sounds like a great idea. I've been a bit of a hermit since I arrived, haven't I?"

Rowan nodded, smiling. "A bit, perhaps."

"I've been a little too enamored of the dungeon," Lorcan said.

Rowan snickered. "I don't have any objection to that, Sir." It didn't seem right to call Lorcan by his name. He went to kneel next to Lorcan's chair. "Those croissants smell really good." He tried for his most appealing expression.

Lorcan shook his head. "What I want to do is drag you upstairs and fuck you into the mattress. Several times. But I'll be good." He tore off a piece of croissant, spread some jam on it then pressed it to Rowan's lips. "Food. Exercise. Then, I think I'll have to torment you a little before we get to the main event."

Rowan tried to concentrate on the buttery flakes dissolving on his tongue. He regretted suggesting a walk, however much he wanted to get to know Lorcan better. There were plenty of flat surfaces in the snug — he wasn't fussy — but now Lorcan was going to draw out the anticipation for far too long. A tug on his hair brought him back to reality.

"Soon, Rowan. It'll be worth the wait. I promise."

Chapter Eight

Rowan had to admit that the grounds of The Retreat were stunning. Covering around forty acres, narrow paths wound through the trees that encircled the property on all sides. Formal gardens were limited to the back of the house and though they were well laid out, Rowan preferred the mysterious atmosphere of the woods. Sunlight broke through the leaves, dappling the paths with light. Some of them were like tunnels with branches arching across them from both sides. Every now and again he caught sight of some small animal scurrying away through the leaf litter and the sound of birdsong mixed with the constant rustle of leaves.

"Where should we go?" asked Lorcan.

"I only arrived here the day before you, Sir," Rowan explained. "I'm afraid I never got the chance to explore the grounds."

"Then we shall just have to go where the paths take us," Lorcan said. "I don't think there's much chance of us getting lost. The boundary wall will always guide us back to the gates. I need to walk off all those croissants you made me eat."

"Me?" Rowan protested. "I think it was you that decided the last one looked lonely on the plate and had to be eaten."

"Tor would have been insulted if we'd left anything and he's ex-military, I wouldn't want to risk annoying him. He might decide to shoot me."

"This isn't America," Rowan said with a giggle. "We don't generally carry guns over here."

"And that's one of the things I love about this country," Lorcan said. "One of the reasons for coming here, apart from visiting The Retreat of course, is for me to find a place to live. I'd like you to help me with that. I've avoided opening my laptop since I arrived, but sooner or later I'm going to have to reconnect with the world. I may have sold my business but I have a lot of other interests that I can't abandon."

"I'd be happy to help," Rowan said. "I know all the property sites. I've been saving up for a deposit on a place of my own since I started work. I'm way off yet, but it's fun to browse through the places for sale. Though I doubt you will be looking at same kind of places as me."

"I'll need a crash pad in London," Lorcan said. "Preferably somewhere within easy reach of The Underground, but that won't be my permanent base. I've lived in San Francisco for the last ten years and though city living has its advantages, I want somewhere quieter."

Rowan's heart rate sped up a little. He loved the idea that Lorcan would not be leaving the country at the end of his stay and maybe, just maybe, there was a minute chance Rowan might get to see more of him beyond The Retreat.

"If you don't mind me asking, Sir, what kind of place did you have in San Francisco? Have you ever been to Alcatraz? And I read about giant redwoods that grow near the Golden Gate Bridge, they must be quite a sight. And have you ever been to the Folsom Street fair? That must be amazing." He realized he had been chattering away, not allowing Lorcan to get a word in edgeways. "Sorry, I've not had the chance to travel for real. I take my trips on the internet and San Francisco is one of the places on my must-visit list."

"I have a house in Pacific Heights, which I spend so little time in I'd be hard pressed to describe some of the rooms. My office has, I mean had, an amazing view of the bridge. And yes, I have been to Folsom a couple of times. There's a great atmosphere. But I've never been to Alcatraz or done any of the tourist spots, which is shameful. But you have to understand, Rowan. My business has been all consuming. There hasn't been space in my life for much else for a long time."

Rowan reached for Lorcan's hand, hoping he wasn't being too forward. Lorcan intertwined their fingers.

"Being here — this break — is the start of a new life with new priorities. I'm in the fortunate position that I can afford the lifestyle I want, where I want, but I'm not the kind of man who is able to sit idle. I have several ideas for new start-ups and investments, so once I'm settled I'll be back at work, though I have no intention of allowing it to take over my life again."

"You should meet my aunt Rory," Rowan said. "She's a lawyer and she works really hard, but she always says that we only have one life to live and that it's okay to be selfish some of the time. Making yourself happy gives you more capacity to make others feel good. I think it's a great philosophy."

"She sounds like an eminently sensible woman."

Rowan pictured his crazy aunt. "I'm not sure anyone would ever apply the word sensible to Rory," he admitted. "She's a little crazy, I have to admit. Do you have much family, Sir?"

Lorcan frowned.

"I'm sorry," Rowan said. "I'm being nosy. It's none of my business."

"No, it's good to be able to talk with someone who has no agenda."

"I kind of do have an agenda," Rowan said, nibbling on his lower lip. "I don't want you to change your mind about fucking me."

Before he knew what was happening, Lorcan had pushed him up against the nearest tree and had pinned his arms above his head. He leaned in for a kiss and Rowan parted his lips in anticipation. Lorcan ravished his mouth in a way that took Rowan's breath away, leaving him gasping and his cock fighting its prison. His skin burned from the rub of Lorcan's stubble. Lorcan held his wrists against the bark for a while longer, staring into his eyes.

"That's not likely to be something I'd forget," he growled. He shoved a hand down the back of Rowan's jeans to grope his arse. "This is mine."

Rowan swallowed. The possession in Lorcan's voice was a huge turn-on. He nodded, his mouth too dry to speak.

"So long as that's understood, let's walk a bit further," Lorcan said, taking Rowan's hand again. "I don't have much family that I know of. Not blood relatives anyway. I was adopted as a baby by a wealthy couple who gave me everything I could ever have wanted, including an exclusive education. But I was only ever an accessory to their lifestyle and I didn't see that much of them when I was growing up. So long as I put in an appearance at various parties and social events, I could do what I pleased. Don't get me wrong, I'm not some poor little rich kid starved of affection. Mom and Dad led very busy lives and they did their best. They were a bit older than most parents because they tried for years to have a child of their own. They've retired to Florida now and spend most of their time on the golf course."

"Do they know…? I mean, have you told them…?"

"That I'm gay?" Lorcan nodded. "I came out when I was sixteen and they couldn't care less. They are fairly liberal. They still expect grandkids at some point because they adopted themselves, so they see no good reason why they can't have them. How about you? Are your parents okay with your orientation?"

"I think they knew before I did," Rowan responded. "When I came out they weren't surprised at all. I think they worry for me, you know, that I'll get myself into trouble I can't get out of with some man, but so far they've been supportive. Mum's waiting for me to bring someone home to dinner but I think that's more because she wants to show off her cooking than meet my boyfriend." He giggled. "She is a fantastic cook, though. She got my friend Ed hooked on baking and now he's a trainee chef at the hotel where I used to work."

"Sounds like we both lucked out on the family front," Lorcan said. To Rowan, he sounded sad, as if talking about his past brought back painful memories. "I think we should be getting back. All this fresh air is going to my head and I'm quite tempted to find a fallen trunk to bend you over."

"I'm not that fond of creepy crawlies." Rowan shivered, imagining what he might come nose to nose with in that scenario.

"Me either. Get going." Lorcan gave Rowan's arse a smack. "The sooner we get back, the sooner we can get to the good stuff."

* * * *

Lorcan gazed out of the circular picture window at the end of the attic. The view was spectacular and he couldn't wait for it to fill Rowan's vision. However, his current companion was Luke Redding, not Rowan.

"I think we are all set," Luke said, making a final adjustment to the equipment he had been preparing. "All you need to do to set the machine going is flick the switch." He demonstrated the device Lorcan had requested, which whirred into life. Lorcan smiled as he watched the fucking machine pump backward and forward. The thick black dildo mounted on the horizontal arm remained steady. He still needed to apply a thick coating of lube but otherwise he was happy with his preparations.

"It only has the one speed," Luke informed him. "And it's probably not fast enough to make a man come, but I imagine that's what you want, isn't it?"

Lorcan nodded. "Rowan is in chastity and he's going to stay that way a bit longer. This scene is the prelude to the main event."

"I'm impressed. This set up is fiendish. I think Rowan will love it."

"I hope so," Lorcan replied. "I want to do something special, so he remembers our first time together."

"I'm glad you took your time before asking him to take the next step with you. As submissives go, Rowan is an innocent and I think he needs time to get things straight in his head before he makes decisions."

"That's an accurate assessment," Lorcan agreed. "And you don't have to worry, Luke. I'll never push him further than I think he can go. The boy's probably never had to use his safe word in his life. I don't intend that he should have to use it with me."

"Good to know." Luke checked his watch. "He'll be here soon, so I'm going to go. Enjoy the rest of the day."

Lorcan spent a few minutes checking the rest of the equipment he and Luke had hauled to the loft. It was the first time Lorcan had been into the space, not having seen it on his tour. It had been kept simple because its main attribute was the view. The A-frames supporting the roof made perfect places for tying or suspending a sub for a good flogging, but Lorcan had other ideas. He was fond of predicament bondage and, after discussing his ideas with Luke, had come up with a suitably wicked plan. While he and Luke had made the arrangements, he had sent Rowan to his room to have a shower and handle other essential matters. Lorcan would have been quite happy to help him with that but he needed time to prepare. He wanted everything ready when Rowan arrived, so that he could enjoy the experience too rather than worry about whether everything was going to work. Luke had been thorough and had even got down on his hands and knees to check the positioning of the machine.

There was a slight creak and Lorcan turned to see Rowan entering the attic through the door at the far end of the roof. He had followed Lorcan's instructions to the letter and was clad only in a black leather jockstrap, which concealed the chastity device imprisoning his cock. Lorcan couldn't wait to see how the black straps framed Rowan's ass once he was down on all fours.

Rowan walked toward him. He was smiling but when he saw the equipment set up on the central path through the attic, his eyes widened. He lost his footing and pitched forward. Lorcan reached him just in time to stop him hitting the floor. He released his hold only when he was certain Rowan wouldn't fall.

"Hello, Rowan." Lorcan greeted him with a smile. "Quite the entrance. I hope you're ready to play."

Rowan nibbled on his lower lip but nodded. There was a flush to his cheeks and his eyes sparkled.

"I'm going to push you hard this afternoon," Lorcan warned. "You are going to be immobilized and at my mercy, so remember your safe words."

Lorcan picked up a pair of steel wrist cuffs joined by a rigid bar. He locked them around Rowan's wrists. Rowan stared at them as if he didn't quite understand how they'd gotten there.

From his pocket, Lorcan extracted a set of nipple clamps connected by a sturdy chain. Each clamp was fixed with four individual screws that would dig into Rowan's tender flesh. Lorcan gave Rowan's nipples a few flicks with his finger, bringing them to hardened peaks. He fixed the clamps in place, tightening the screws until Rowan squirmed and panted. Lorcan gave the chain an experimental tug, making Rowan moan. The sound made Lorcan hard. The afternoon was going to be just as much of a trial for him as it was for Rowan.

"You see the foam pad down there on the floor? I want you to position yourself in the middle of it, on your hands and knees."

The pad was made of memory foam, meaning that Rowan's knees would be comfortable, even if the rest of him wasn't. Rowan got into place and Lorcan took a moment to admire the firm globes of his ass.

"Have you heard of predicament bondage, Rowan?"

"Yes, Sir."

"It's one of my favorite ways to play." Lorcan collected the two spreader bars he had waiting. The first went between Rowan's knees, with the straps fastened just above the joint, pushing his thighs apart. The second bar, which was slightly longer, Lorcan placed between his ankles. He made sure the cuffs were tight, not wanting them to chafe. He then took a link chain with clips at either end. One clip was fastened to the bar between Rowan's knees the other to the center of the chain linking his nipple clamps.

"I suggest you put your forearms flat on the floor. It will make your position more stable." Lorcan waited until Rowan was in place then tied a strip of black silk around his eyes. "The sensations you feel will be magnified without your sight."

Lorcan applied lube to the dildo that was now pointing directly at Rowan's hole. The height setting was perfect so Lorcan didn't have to make any last-minute adjustments. He slicked his fingers and pressed two of them to Rowan's ass. Rowan jerked forward at the contact and gasped.

"As you've just discovered," Lorcan said, "if you remain in position and keep still, the tension on the chain remains slack. But the moment you try to pull away it will go taut and tug on your nipples." He pushed his fingers into Rowan's channel, stretching him quickly. The process wasn't about giving Rowan pleasure, just making him ready for the machine. The dildo wasn't as big as Lorcan's cock but sizeable enough for Rowan to feel it. Satisfied that he had prepared Rowan enough, Lorcan wiped his hands on a cloth. He moved the fucking machine closer to Rowan so that the tip of the dildo pressed against his hole. He held it in place then flicked the switch to turn the machine on. With slow but inexorable pressure, the machine pushed the dildo into Rowan's body. Rowan's entire frame shivered. His immediate response was to try to get away from the intrusion by edging forward. The resulting tug on the nipple clamps brought him straight back into position.

"Oh my God," Rowan moaned. "It's so much... I can't..."

"You can." Lorcan spoke with absolute certainty. He watched, entranced, as the machine fucked his helpless sub. Retraction of the machine's arm meant that the dildo was pulled completely from Rowan's body before being pressed back inside. Rowan whimpered and panted, his breath coming in short gasps. Watching him turned Lorcan's erection to iron. He went to stand in front of Rowan's head then pulled off the blindfold. Rowan's eyes were glazed and Lorcan wasn't sure how much he was seeing as he unzipped his fly and pulled out his aching dick. He palmed himself, hefting the weight of his shaft before rubbing his thumb over the sticky head.

"Please, Sir..." Rowan's line of sight was firmly fixed on Lorcan's groin. Lorcan jacked himself slowly, not wanting to come too soon.

"What is it, Rowan?" Lorcan didn't expect an answer. He jacked his hand faster, getting rougher, bringing himself to the edge of orgasm. He came and splatters of white liquid landed on Rowan's face. Rowan licked his lips, gathering as much of Lorcan's cum as he could. Lorcan leaned against the roof supports, legs a bit unsteady. He rested there, recovering, while the inexorable machine — that had no problems with fatigue — continued to drill into Rowan's hole.

Rowan began to tremble and Lorcan decided he had had enough. He switched off the machine then released Rowan from the spreader bars as quickly as he could. The linking chain connected to the nipple clamps followed. He brought Rowan to his feet, keeping a protective arm around his shoulders while he loosened the screws on the clamps. As they came free, Rowan screamed, his voice ragged. Lorcan rubbed the soreness away then pulled him into a hug, Rowan's bound hands trapped between them. He whispered soothing, nonsense words into Rowan's ear and planted soft kisses on his hot skin.

"I'm proud of you," he murmured. "You were spectacular."

Rowan nestled against him and kept as close as he could while Lorcan guided him down the stairs from the attic back to the Blue Room. Once inside, he lifted Rowan onto the bed, leaving him there for just a moment while he fetched a warm, damp flannel from the bathroom. He wiped Rowan's face before fetching him a bottle of water and supported him while he drank.

"Lie there and rest," Lorcan said. He stripped out of his clothes before joining Rowan, pulling him close. He stroked Rowan's back and listened to his soft sighs as he relaxed. "That was quite the afternoon, wasn't it? Something we'll both remember for a while."

Lorcan closed his eyes, feeling drowsy. A nap seemed like a good idea. He drifted into sleep to the sound of Rowan's breathing.

* * * *

Rowan awoke to warmth and a dreamy sense of inner satisfaction. He tried to roll over but found himself contained in a prison formed by Lorcan's arms. Disorientation swamped him and for a moment he had no idea where he was or what time of day it was. Lorcan shifted, tightening his grip. Rowan grinned — even in sleep, Lorcan was overprotective. Gradually, the events of the day seeped into Rowan's consciousness. He wondered if it had all been a dream. The scene Lorcan had gone to so much trouble to set up had pressed every single one of Rowan's submissive buttons. After only a week together, it seemed Lorcan knew him better than he knew himself.

Beneath the covers he fingered the infuriating plastic encasing his cock.

"Leave it alone. That belongs to me." Lorcan's voice was rough from sleep.

"Did today really happen?" Rowan asked.

"I believe it's still happening. How long have we been asleep?"

Rowan peered at the clock on the dresser. "I'm not sure what time we came back to the room, but it's five o'clock now."

"Just an hour or so, then." Lorcan stretched and the covers drifted down to his waist.

Feeling brave, Rowan planted a gentle kiss on the hard planes of Lorcan's chest.

"It's been a wonderful day. I'll never forget it."

"I would hope not. But it's not over yet." Lorcan slipped out of bed, much to Rowan's disappointment. He tried to see what he was doing but there wasn't much light under the four-poster and the curtains were partly drawn. He settled for admiring the lines of Lorcan's naked body. He was erect and his cock bobbed as he returned to the bed, something clasped in his hand. Lorcan pulled the covers to the foot of the bed, leaving Rowan exposed before climbing up next to him.

"I'm not going to tease you," Lorcan said. From his hand he produced a condom and the key to Rowan's chastity device. With a few deft movements, he removed it. Rowan's cock stiffened with alarming speed.

"It doesn't seem to have done you any harm." Lorcan petted Rowan's aching shaft.

"Sir…please! If you keep touching me I'll come!"

"Well, we can't have that. Not yet. Not until I'm inside you. Turn over." Lorcan switched his attention to Rowan's backside, fingering his hole. "Still nice and slick. You're not sore after this afternoon?"

"Not at all. Just empty, Sir." Rowan knew there was a note of pleading in his voice. He couldn't help himself. He wanted Lorcan inside him with quiet desperation. Nothing else was acceptable.

"I want you looking into my eyes when we make love for the first time," Lorcan said.

Tears welled and Rowan snuffled while he shifted onto his back. Lorcan brushed a tear away.

"No more words." He rolled on a condom then lifted Rowan's legs so his calves rested on Lorcan's shoulders.

Rowan held his breath. The moment he'd dreamed about was finally happening. When Lorcan pushed inside him, a piece of a puzzle Rowan hadn't even realized was missing slid into place. Sheer joy ignited every single nerve ending Rowan possessed and he sighed his contentment. Lorcan smiled down at him, holding his weight on his arms.

"You good?"

"Perfect."

"Thank Christ!" Lorcan pumped his hips, no longer holding back. He was an aggressive lover, claiming Rowan's body with fierce determination. There was no way Rowan could prevent the orgasm that rolled through him. After almost a week in chastity, his body was no longer under his control. His vision grayed and though he was aware of Lorcan driving into him, he could do nothing but lie there and take what Lorcan gave him. He spurted his release between their bodies, hips jerking, muscles in spasm. Lorcan lowered one of his legs to the bed then twisted him to the side, gaining deeper penetration. Rowan's orgasm continued. It was too much. Lorcan came, straining inside him. Rowan screamed Lorcan's name then the world faded to black.

It couldn't have been many minutes later when Rowan regained consciousness to find Lorcan wiping him clean. The scent of their lovemaking filled the air. Rowan breathed deeply, not wanting to forget a single moment. He lost his breath to Lorcan's kiss, parting his lips to accept Lorcan's tongue. He tasted him back, surprised at his own temerity, and Lorcan responded with a fierceness that made Rowan's heart pound. The kiss left him no room to doubt who had control.

Lorcan rolled onto his back, one arm beneath his head. He pulled Rowan close before Rowan could regret the loss of contact.

"Next time, I'm going to tie you down. Fuck you long and slow until you scream in frustration."

Rowan was just happy there was going to be a next time. He snuggled against Lorcan's warm, firm body.

"Yes, Sir." He hoped it wouldn't be too long before Lorcan lived up to his words.

"I'm going to plug you, dress you in nothing but a leather collar and cuffs, then have you kneel next to me through dinner. I want you to keep yourself hard. By the time I take you to bed again this evening you'll be mad with need."

Rowan squirmed, his cock already plumping into life.

"That sounds wonderful, Sir."

Lorcan chuckled. "You might not be saying that in a few hours' time. I think my more sadistic tendencies need an airing."

"I'm at your service." Rowan rubbed his cock against Lorcan's thigh in an attempt to get some friction.

"And I think we will start with a nice, spiked cock ring."

Rowan's moan was a mixture of dread and anticipation. He suspected he still had plenty to learn about Lorcan and that those lessons were likely to be frustrating in the extreme. He gave a contented sigh. It was hard to imagine how life could get any better.

Chapter Nine

Rowan wished he had a softer chair. Working on the big table in the banqueting hall gave him the space he needed to spread out his paperwork, but the eighteenth-century dining set had not been built for comfort. He shifted from one cheek to the other but only succeeded in jiggling the end of the plug lodged in his arse. He was grateful that Lorcan had replaced the spiked cock ring he had been using for the last few days in favor of one made of leather, but the ball splitter was hard to ignore, especially since Rowan was naked. Lorcan seemed to have developed an aversion to Rowan wearing any clothes at all, apart from a matched set of red leather cuffs around his wrists and ankles and a narrow collar. The house was warm but Rowan would have preferred to be a little less exposed. Not that anyone on the staff looked at him as if his condition was anything other than normal. Today, though, it didn't seem fair. Lorcan had left for London early that morning, leaving Rowan with a list of instructions, the first of which was to remain naked. He had actually handwritten the list, with 'stay naked' written in block capitals on the first line.

The next instruction was much more enjoyable. Lorcan had asked him to start building a portfolio of potential properties for him to view both in London and in the Cotswolds. In the capital, Lorcan had specified that the property should be within a twenty-minute walk of The Underground. He also had some stringent security requirements and a preference for a top-floor apartment. He didn't want a house because the place in London would be more of a crash pad than anything. He had been less specific about the house in the country, leaving it to Rowan to make some suggestions. He did want enough space for a playroom and again, security was important to him, though he was content to have systems installed if need be.

Rowan had spent a very enjoyable couple of hours viewing luxury properties on all the upmarket estate agents' websites. When he found a place he thought might appeal to Lorcan, he printed off the details. He also bookmarked all the pages in case Lorcan wanted to look at them online. Luke had helped him set up a printer on the table so he had everything he needed. *Except a cushion.* At eleven, Tor brought him cookies and milk from the kitchen. He returned again at one with a plate of sandwiches and some sliced fruit. By the time he had eaten, Rowan was ready for a break. He tidied his papers then made the short trip to his room, hoping to be able to make a couple of phone calls. He hadn't had a chance to call home or talk to Ed for several days.

He sat on his bed, Bilbo on the pillow next to him. Even though he was alone and in his own space, he didn't dress. Lorcan's orders had been clear and Rowan had no intention of disobeying him. He called Rory first in the hope that she might be working from home and she answered on the first ring.

"Rowan, you wicked boy, why haven't you called me?"

Rowan held the handset away from his ear.

"I've been kind of tied up," he said, trying not to laugh.

"I don't think I want to know. I know you said it might be a while before you'd be able to call, but it's been ages. You're lucky I didn't send the cavalry down there to rescue you."

"I don't need rescuing," Rowan reassured her. "I love the job and the place is amazing. The client is…demanding, but nothing I can't handle. He's American and has a wonderful accent. I like him, Rory. I like him a lot."

"You're falling for him." Rory's statement sounded like an accusation. "Be careful, Rowan. I don't want you hurt."

"I won't be. I know he's only here for four weeks and then he'll go back to his world, which is so far away from mine you wouldn't believe. But he's patient with me. Firm but kind. I know where I stand with him and the other staff here are great. It's kind of like a family."

"Well, I'm glad it's working out for you, but I'll still be pleased to see you back here when you get your break. You are coming back, aren't you?"

"Of course! I can't wait to see you. And Ed of course — he texts every day, mainly with descriptions of the things he's been cooking. I'm going to call him next. I'll probably get an earful of abuse."

"If he's been hearing from you as little as I have, I don't blame him," Rory said. "It's a shame you can't tell me who the client is because then I could find his email address and send him abusive notes."

Rowan giggled. "And that's probably one of the reasons why the security here is so strict — to avoid hate mail from rabid relatives."

"Rabid? Did you just compare me to a diseased dog? If you're not careful, your arse will get another spanking when you get back here, cheeky boy."

Rowan rang off with Rory's raucous laughter echoing in his ears. He called Ed next, hoping that he'd be done with lunch service at the hotel, but got his voicemail. He left a short message and promised to ring back as soon as he could. There wasn't anyone else he wanted to call, so he lay back on his bed with his arms behind his head. He missed Lorcan. He felt a bit aimless without his Dom there to guide him. Written instructions weren't the same as Lorcan's commanding tones. He wondered what Lorcan was doing in London and whether Rayne's chatter had driven him mad yet. He was a little envious that his friend got to spend the day with Lorcan instead of him, but he couldn't be mad at Rayne. He hadn't had much chance to chat with the young chauffeur, but Rayne was always ready with a smile and an encouraging word when they crossed paths. Lorcan hadn't used his services very often so Rowan guessed that Rayne would have been glad for something to do, even if it had meant getting up at the crack of dawn.

Peering down his body, Rowan tried to get of decent view of his cock and balls. The leather splitter stretched his skin taut and had the effect of making everything stick out more than usual. He had almost come when

Lorcan had fastened the straps in place, which had earned him extra spanks. His cock twitched at the memory. He decided it was time to get back to work because if he carried on daydreaming, he'd just get harder and more frustrated. He returned to the banqueting hall where he poked his tongue out at the hard chair. He thought he'd done enough property research. Until he had the chance to go through his choices with Lorcan, he could only guess at his preferences. He had already cleaned and tidied the Blue Room so he checked the next item on his list.

"Explore the other bedrooms and choose a new place for tonight's scene. I can do that." He wandered through to the hall then up the sweeping staircase to the landing. The Blue Room was first on the left so Rowan decided to work his way round from there. He'd seen all the rooms before but Lorcan kept him so busy that he hadn't been back and he wanted to remind himself of each one before making a decision. The room next to the blue one had a dark red theme, with gold highlights in the soft furnishings and heavy drapes. Chunky mahogany furniture complemented the color scheme and the bathroom was all dramatic black tile and mirrors. The bed wasn't a full four-poster, but had tall pillars at each corner. Rowan could easily imagine himself spread-eagled on the sumptuous quilt, chained in place, though he thought that might be a bit tame for Lorcan. There were two special features in the room — the first was a wooden chest that sat at the foot of the bed. A concealed drawer in its base held two telescopic steel poles that slotted into holes in the corners of the chest and sloped at an angle to form a V shape. Cuffs at the end of each pole meant that a man could be restrained lying flat on his back on the cushioned lid of the chest with his legs held in a splayed, vertical position leaving his arse exposed for whatever his master desired. It was an ingenious design. Rowan gave the padded top an experimental prod to test how well cushioned it was. It had potential. The room's second secret was a cage concealed beneath the bed, the bars covered by a fabric skirt. There was only enough room for a man to lie flat and Rowan imagined that he would feel claustrophobic if he had to spend any time in the space.

He moved onto the next room where he remembered there was a priest's secret hideaway. Underneath an ornate Turkish rug, a trapdoor lifted to reveal what was little more than a hole in the floor. Bars had been added across the top and holes drilled in the trapdoor. It meant that the cage roof could be left exposed, or a prisoner could be kept in virtual darkness if the trapdoor was lowered. Rowan shivered. He didn't like the idea of being confined in such a small space. He put everything back in place quickly and walked across to a room-height mirror set on the wall. It took him a few seconds to locate the button that activated a mechanism which swiveled the mirror through one hundred and eighty degrees to reveal a padded surface, holding a lattice of bungee cords attached to hooks. Every limb could be held in place by the network of straps. More could be placed across the chest, shoulders and neck. He pulled on one of the cords, noting the limited elasticity. A man held in place by the full array would be completely trapped — like prey in a spider's web. He could picture the marks that would be left on his body. It was the perfect bondage to keep a sub still for further torment. Rowan thought that Lorcan would probably like it a lot, but the priest's cage put Rowan off. He put the Gold Room on his reserve list.

The next room, with its cool gray theme, was more modern than the others. It was full of tactile fabrics in dark gray and purple shades but the furniture was beech, much paler than in the other rooms. The king-sized bed had a heavy wooden footboard with concealed hinges. Sections of the wood could be removed to make holes, creating an ingenious set of stocks. One hole was big enough for a man's neck, the others for his ankles. It was possible to restrain somebody either lying horizontal on the bed or on the floor with legs raised.

The second secret appeared to be a coat stand but its base was weighted, making it difficult to move. The pegs attached to its central length were adjustable, offering a variety of bondage positions. It was intriguing, but Rowan didn't find it particularly exciting. He went on to the Green Room on the opposite side of the landing. This was Rowan's second favorite. He loved the deep green décor and polished oak furniture. There was also a gorgeous sunken bath and multi-headed shower.

The concealed toys in the green room made his cock jerk. The first was simple—an armchair with a seat that flipped over to reveal a fixed dildo. The thought of being bound to the chair, impaled on the toy made Rowan want to rip off his cock ring and bring himself to orgasm as quickly as possible. Two simple snap fastenings were all that stood between him and release. He gripped his right wrist with his left hand behind his back, squeezing hard enough to hurt. The pain gave him a measure of control.

When he had explored the room for the first time it had taken him a while to work out where the other secrets were hidden. In one corner of the room, hanging from a sturdy chain, was an ornate birdcage big enough to house a large parrot. When he had looked closely he had realized that the floor of the cage was a horseshoe-shaped cushion of padded leather with a hole in the middle and that a section of the cage beneath the door was cut out. It meant that a man could sit suspended above the floor with his upper body trapped in the cage and his arse exposed from below. The cage could be lowered and raised using a pulley concealed behind a curtain.

Rowan brushed his hand over the polished surface of a saddle stand that doubled as a clothes rack. Only some brass D-rings laid into the wood revealed that the piece of furniture wasn't quite what it seemed. The apex of the stand was a triangular ridge and if a man were made to straddle it, he would have to stand on tiptoe to avoid painful pressure on his balls and hole as the wood pressed between his arse cheeks. Rowan measured its height against his own body and judged that there would be little he could do to avoid resting his weight on the sharp angle.

"Definitely this room," he murmured. He checked everything over to make sure there was no need to clean but the room was immaculate. He opened the window a crack to let in some fresh air then left. It was heading toward dinnertime and Rowan had no idea when Lorcan was due back. A brief pang of loneliness struck him and he decided to go to the small breakroom off the kitchen to see if either of Tor's assistants might be around to chat over a cup of coffee. As he crossed the hall, Luke appeared from his office, moving silently as always.

"I'm glad I caught you, Rowan. Rayne just called to let me know that Mr. Wilder is on his way back and he'd like you to arrange dinner for seven-thirty."

"Yes, Mr. Redding. That's only a little later than usual so I hope it won't upset Tor's plans too much."

"I'm sure he'll accommodate Mr. Wilder," Luke said. "You may also be relieved to know that he said you should dress for dinner. Your choice of outfit. And remove the collar and cuffs you have on."

Rowan had grown accustomed to wandering around the house naked but he was glad to scuttle back to his room and pick out some clothes. He selected a pair of supple leather trousers with a placket that could be removed, turning them into a pair of chaps, and a cream, cotton shirt with loose sleeves and mother-of-pearl buttons that glimmered in the light. The fabric was translucent so his nipples were visible through the fabric. He didn't bother with footwear because he didn't need it in the house and Lorcan preferred him barefoot. He applied a slick of clear lip gloss and highlighted his eyes with liner. A little product in his hair and he was ready.

He decided that a trip to the kitchen was still a good idea. A cup of coffee would ensure he stayed alert for the evening, and able to focus on Lorcan's pleasure. When he got to the staff room he was pleased to find Benjy and Frank already at the table, a huge chocolate cake between them.

"Rowan!" Frank said. "Your timing is perfect. We're just about to test this cake."

"Tor made it for us," Benjy added. "As a reward for being good."

"It's strange to see you with your clothes on." Frank giggled. "Not that we don't enjoy the view."

"It's a perk of the job," Benjy declared. "I hope no one wants us to cook naked because that would be…dangerous!"

"But we would…if we had to." Frank grinned. He picked up a knife that wouldn't have been out of place in a *Scream* movie then used it to carve out three slices of cake.

"I came down in the hope of coffee," Rowan said. The cake, sandwiched with cream and jam, made his mouth water.

"There's a fresh pot over there. I just brewed it." Benjy pointed at the percolator. "Bring the jug and some mugs. We can all have some."

Rowan fetched everything they needed, collecting a container of milk from the fridge.

"I only have about half an hour before Mr. Wilder gets back. I shouldn't eat too much because I'll have dinner with him later."

Benjy poured the coffee. "We're kind of jealous. Mr. Wilder is an eleven on the hotness scale. We don't get much Dommy action in the kitchen apart from watching Chef."

"Who I would climb like a tree," Frank said, shoving cake into his mouth. "Oh, God, this is so good."

"You can have Chef and I'll have Mr. Redding," Benjy said. "He's sooo scary. I'll bet he spanks really hard."

Rowan listened to their banter with a smile. They had a similar camaraderie to him and Ed, albeit in a different context.

"I have to admit, they are both gorgeous."

"But you get to play with Mr. Wilder and he's scrummier than this cake."

"If you had my job, you wouldn't get to cook though," Rowan said.

Benjy and Frank shared a glance. Benjy pouted. "Not an option. We love to cook and we get to do things here that we couldn't at The Underground."

"And Chef is patient most of the time. He's only whacked my arse with a spatula a few times," Frank said, grinning.

"And threatened to make us both work wearing ball gags if we don't shut up," Benjy added.

Rowan laughed. "You two are great therapy. My best friend Ed is a trainee chef. You guys remind me of him." He glanced at the clock on the wall. "I have to go! Thanks for the cake." He got hugs from both sides.

"Come visit again soon."

"I will."

Rowan made his way back to the hall, eager to see Lorcan. There was none of the worry he'd had on their first meeting, just excited anticipation. He peeked out of the door to find a thick drizzle soaking the gardens and shrouding everything in gloom. He retreated to the hall and picked a position facing the entrance then settled onto his knees to wait. Clasping his hands behind his back, he lowered his head and slowed his breathing. He registered Luke leaving his office but didn't look up. A draught from the door ruffled Rowan's hair and he guessed Luke had gone to wait outside. He was a little jealous that Luke would get to see Lorcan before he did but then the crunch of tires over gravel cleared his mind of everything except Lorcan's return. The murmur of voices outside let him know that Luke was talking to Lorcan about something. Then the door banged open and two sets of footsteps came inside. Rowan badly wanted to peek from beneath his lashes but he remained still. Just in front of his knees he could see the toe caps of a pair of brown leather boots and the frayed hems of a pair of blue jeans. Lorcan. Rowan's cock jerked.

"Have you been good for me today, Rowan?" Lorcan put a finger beneath Rowan's chin, tilting his head back. "I do hope so. After being apart all day, I'd hate to have to punish you."

"I…"

"Hush." Lorcan brought Rowan to his feet. "One look into your pretty eyes tells me what I need to know. You'll never be able to hide anything from me."

"I missed you, Sir." Rowan wasn't sure whether it was appropriate to admit to that, but the words just slipped out. Lorcan's expression softened.

"I missed you too. It's been a long day and all the way back from London in the car I've been looking forward to spending time with you."

Rowan's cheeks heated and he felt shy, not wanting to make eye contact with Lorcan in case he gave something away about his developing feelings. Lorcan wasn't going to let him off the hook so easily, though.

"Look at me."

Rowan raised his eyes to find Lorcan smiling. He tilted his head in hope of a kiss and was rewarded with a firm press of Lorcan's lips. The kiss was unhurried, undemanding and tender. Rowan didn't want it to end but it had to.

"Was Rayne good company today, Sir?" Rowan asked.

"That boy needs a permanent gag, but he's a good driver and he knows his way around the city."

Rowan giggled. Lorcan wasn't the type for idle chatter.

"I put my headphones in and I don't think he even noticed." Lorcan's expression was comical. "He probably kept talking to himself even when I was in meetings."

"That wouldn't surprise me at all, Sir. Is there anything I can do for you before dinner? Would you like to freshen up, or rest?"

"Strangely, I'm not tired but I will take a quick shower and change my clothes before we eat. You look spectacular by the way. After dinner, I want you to show me which of the bedrooms you've chosen for us to use. I know you've been working hard on your property research, but that can wait until tomorrow morning."

Lorcan took Rowan's hand then led him up the stairs to the Blue Room. As soon as they were inside the door, shut away from the rest of the world, Lorcan pushed Rowan against the wall. He unfastened the placket on his trousers, freeing his cock.

"This hasn't been giving you any trouble, has it?" he asked, releasing the snaps on the cock ring and ball splitter.

"No, Sir. It wasn't too tight. It didn't affect my circulation. I kind of liked the way it felt," Rowan admitted.

"I love the way it looked on you." Lorcan fondled Rowan's balls. Rowan's breath hitched.

"I'll come, Sir."

"Yes, you will." Lorcan's grin was feral. He continued his manipulations and Rowan couldn't help but thrust into his hand. He didn't know what he had done to deserve such a treat but he didn't dare say anything in case Lorcan stopped. He pressed his shoulders into the wall for support, his legs shaking. Lorcan rubbed his thumb over the head of Rowan's cock before digging his nail into the slit. The moment of sharp pain took Rowan over the edge and he shot into Lorcan's hand with a moan. The orgasm left him panting, unable to catch his breath. Lorcan guided him to the bed where he managed to lie down in an uncoordinated sprawl.

"You can stay there for a few minutes, while I take a shower."

Rowan mumbled something in response but the words didn't make sense. His jumbled thoughts resisted any attempt to organize them into something coherent. Lorcan had made sure their evening got off to an amazing start and Rowan couldn't wait for the rest of it to play out.

Chapter Ten

"You chose the perfect room, Rowan." Lorcan ran a hand over the saddle stand. "I think we'll start here and, much as I love those pants, I'd be much happier if you were naked, so strip. Slowly."

Lorcan chose to sit in an armchair in the corner of the room while Rowan removed his clothes. The room was lit by a single lamp, the light catching on Rowan's shirt buttons and the golden highlights in his hair, holding Lorcan's attention until Rowan began to undress. He took off the shirt first, sliding each button free with shaking fingers. From the flush on his cheekbones, Lorcan guessed the tremors came from excitement rather than nerves. Rowan folded his shirt, placing it on the bed, and Lorcan had a chance to admire his sleek torso and lightly defined muscles. His dark nipples, which had been visible through the fabric of his shirt, were already peaked. Lorcan could picture them adorned with gold rings, perfect for tugging on.

"Have you ever thought about getting some piercings?" he asked. Rowan's fingers strayed toward his chest but he didn't touch.

"I don't think I'm brave enough, Sir."

"Oh, you are. Just think how much fun we would have if I could tug on those sensitive little nubs. I'd decorate your body for my pleasure. Another ring through that tender spot just behind your balls would be perfect."

Rowan's eyes widened. "I..." He moved his legs closer together, placing a splayed hand over his leather-covered crotch.

Lorcan chuckled. "Don't worry, I don't have a piercing kit hidden in my back pocket. You're safe for now."

Rowan's ragged sigh of relief amused Lorcan no end and when Rowan removed his trousers, his erection told Lorcan that he might not be quite as averse to the idea as he pretended. Lorcan filed the information away for future reference.

"Display position." Lorcan snapped out the order. He waited until Rowan stood with his fingers laced behind his head, legs spread, before rising from his chair. Unadorned in any way, Rowan was a canvas ready to be painted with Lorcan's marks, decorated with symbols of his ownership. He buckled a stiff leather collar around Rowan's neck, checking the fit to make sure it wasn't too tight.

"You'll have to keep your head up wearing this. It's called a posture collar. I found it in the dungeon. It looks good on you."

Rowan nibbled on his lower lip, shifting his stance a little. His cock bobbed. Lorcan wrapped his hand around the warm shaft.

"This is mine." The words came out in a growl. "For tonight and until the end of my stay, you belong to me, Rowan. Do you understand?"

"Yes, I understand, Sir."

Lorcan stroked Rowan's smooth skin from shoulder to hip, claiming possession of his body. He dragged a finger between plump ass cheeks, grazing Rowan's hole.

"I really noticed the noise in London today," Lorcan remarked. "It's constant, a kind of rumbling that never goes away. There is noise here, too, of course, but it's gentler and inside, the silence in the house wraps around me like a blanket. I've craved quiet for so long."

He tapped Rowan's arms, encouraging him to lower them to his sides, then pressed close to his back. He enclosed Rowan in a cage of his arms, placing one hand, fingers splayed, across his flat belly. He was taller than Rowan with a heavier frame — it gave him a sense of power, knowing that he was stronger.

"I'm going to gag you this evening. Maintain the silence." He moved his hand toward Rowan's groin, pleased to feel smooth skin beneath his fingertips. "You shaved for me."

"Yes, Sir. It's more comfortable than stubble. I kind of like the way it feels."

"Me too." Lorcan indulged himself with some groping. He squeezed Rowan's rigid shaft, then his heavy balls. "You don't have permission to come."

Rowan's anguished squeak sent a thrill of sadistic pleasure down Lorcan's spine.

"I think we should try out some of the treats this room has to offer, don't you? Go and straddle the clothes stand. I think that will keep you focused while I pick out a gag." He gave Rowan's ass a pat.

Rowan walked slowly over to the saddle stand. He had to go up on his tiptoes to get into position with one leg on either side of the stand. Lorcan arranged him so that his balls rested on the apex of the wood, which also nestled between Rowan's ass cheeks. If he stayed on his toes, the pressure wouldn't be too bad, but if he placed his feet flat on the ground the wood would dig into his tender parts. Rowan rested his hands on the wood front of him, balancing his weight. Lorcan frowned. He went to the toy chest and found a length of rawhide.

"Hands behind your back, Rowan." He bound Rowan's wrists together then tied the loose end of the rawhide to the back of his collar, so that his hands rested mid back, his elbows bent. There was no way Rowan could now use them to alleviate his predicament.

"Much better." Lorcan watched as Rowan struggled to maintain a position that didn't cause him too much discomfort. Sooner or later he'd be forced to stand flat. Lorcan wondered if the pain would make him come. He imagined it might.

He returned to the toy chest and pulled out a selection of gags. He wasn't particularly fond of drool, so rejected the bigger ball gags. There were two options that appealed to him. One was a leather contraption that would cover the bottom half of Rowan's face and buckle at the front. Inside the padded leather, a bulbous rubber piece would fill Rowan's mouth. The second was a bit gag but because it looked to be more uncomfortable, Lorcan opted for the first one. Rowan would be wearing it for a while.

Lorcan fitted the gag while Rowan struggled to maintain his balance. When Lorcan tightened the buckle across his face, Rowan lost his fight. His feet went flat and he moaned into the leather as the wooden ridge pressed into his balls and arse. He tried to rise onto his toes again but his legs were shaking and he failed. Lorcan looked him straight in the eye and smiled.

"Shake your head if you want to use your safe word."

Rowan's erection hadn't flagged and the gleam of pre-cum gave away how close he was to disobedience. Lorcan's sense of satisfaction deepened. He took the chair that sat next to a low table and dragged it to the center of the room, positioning it in Rowan's line of sight. He remembered this toy well because it featured on The Retreat's internet site. He flipped the seat over, revealing the fixed dildo, then locked it into place. A thick coating of lube made the black silicon glisten. Lorcan cleaned his hands then made sure he had enough straps to bind Rowan in place.

"I think I'm ready." He released Rowan's hands then helped him shuffled backward until he was free of the saddle stand. Rowan's eyes glittered and behind the gag he made the sweetest whimpering noises.

"Onto the bed, Rowan," Lorcan ordered. He pressed the jar of lube into Rowan's hand. "Get yourself ready for the chair."

Rowan crawled onto the bed. He stayed on his knees while he slicked two fingers then pressed them into his ass. His muffled moans made Lorcan's cock ache. Watching Rowan prepare himself was the best kind of show.

"That's enough." Lorcan extended a hand and helped Rowan off the bed. He led him to the chair. "Take a seat."

In gradual increments, Rowan lowered himself onto the glistening dildo. His eyes widened as the sizeable toy penetrated his channel. By the time he was fully seated, his eyes were squeezed closed.

"Remember," Lorcan said. "Shake your head if you want this to end. Look at me, Rowan."

Rowan opened his eyes, holding himself absolutely still as if not wanting to risk Lorcan misinterpreting a movement as a wish to stop.

Lorcan used a series of buckled straps to bind Rowan to the chair. They went around his ankles and calves, his waist and chest. His arms were pulled back behind the chair then tied together using the rawhide thong. Lorcan wished he had a camera to take a picture of the image he had created. Knowing that Rowan was impaled by the dildo, even though it couldn't be seen, kept him hard as steel. He stripped, relishing the cool air against his skin. His self-control was fading but he was determined not to come until Rowan's ass was available to him.

He fetched a small crop from the toy box. It was flexible, with a stiff square of leather on the end. He slapped it against his thigh, the sharp sting heightening his senses.

"I wonder how many blows you can take without coming."

Lorcan flicked his wrist, and the crop caught Rowan's left nipple. He concentrated the next few blows in the same spot then moved to the other side of Rowan's chest. Pink bloomed across his pale skin. Lorcan aimed the crop at Rowan's abs, then his thighs and calves. He saved the best target for last. As the first smack hit Rowan's cock, he came, muscles straining against every strap. Lorcan tapped his balls lightly, making him spasm again and again until he was drained. Rowan's head dropped as far as it could in the punishing collar, his skin gleaming with perspiration. Slowly, Lorcan released him from bondage. He lifted Rowan from the chair, scooping his limp body into his arms, before carrying him to the bed. Once Rowan was safely horizontal, Lorcan removed the gag and the collar.

"Sir..." Rowan's voice was little more than a croak. "Please, hold me."

"Water first." Lorcan fetched a bottle from the fridge, unscrewed the cap then supported Rowan's head while he drank. When he had slaked his thirst, Lorcan climbed onto the bed next to him, after slipping a condom beneath his pillow. Rowan clung to him, squirming until he was lying on top of him and they were pressed together chest to chest, Rowan's head resting on Lorcan's shoulder. Lorcan petted Rowan's sweat-dampened hair.

Rowan took a few shuddering breaths then, to Lorcan's surprise, moved to kneel across his thighs before lowering himself onto Lorcan's erection.

"Sorry, Sir. Need you in me. You can punish me later."

"No condom." Lorcan couldn't bear the idea of making Rowan move.

"I know. I want this."

Lorcan didn't argue. They'd seen each other's medical records. He couldn't remain still—he gripped Rowan's hips and turned them over. He wanted Rowan under him. Bending Rowan's knees back, Lorcan drove into his body with a desperate need for release. It didn't take long. The heat and grip of Rowan's channel were too much to resist. Lorcan came hard, tremors running from the base of his skull to his ass. He collapsed onto Rowan's pliant body, rolling them over again before he could crush him. A wave of exhaustion consumed him and, with Rowan snuggled against him, he let sleep drag him under.

* * * *

Rowan sat bolt upright, heart pounding. He stared at his unfamiliar surroundings and when he caught sight of the saddle stand, his discarded leather trousers flung across it, memories of the previous night came flooding back. He grinned. The scene had been better than his wildest imaginings, something he'd never forget. He glanced at the clock, shocked to see that it was almost eleven. He hadn't given the kitchen any information about Lorcan's plans for the day. Tor was going to be furious.

"I can almost hear the cogs whirring." Lorcan yawned. "What time is it?"

"Nearly eleven, Sir." Rowan nibbled his lip. "I'm sorry—I haven't made any arrangements for breakfast."

"Is that what you're worried about?"

Rowan yelped as he was pulled into an embrace. Lorcan's stubble grazed his cheek.

"That's easily dealt with." Lorcan picked up the phone next to the bed. "What's the number for the kitchen?"

"Two, Sir."

Lorcan pressed the button. "Good morning, Tor. I'm afraid I am the reason Rowan neglected his duties last night. Do you think you could see your way to feeding us?" Lorcan winked at Rowan. "That would be perfect. We're in the Green Room. Thanks, Tor, you're a life saver." He replaced the receiver. "Tor's going to send one of the boys up in a while with brunch."

"Oh, what a great idea. I should get up…"

"You're staying right here." Lorcan tightened his grip. "I'm here to be pampered and if I want to keep you in my bed for the entire day then that's where you'll stay."

"Yes, Sir." Rowan was more than happy to be held prisoner in Lorcan's bed. Feeling bold, he ran his hand down Lorcan's chest then beneath the covers to his cock.

"You're treading on dangerous ground," Lorcan warned. "You must be sore from yesterday evening."

"A little," Rowan admitted. "My lips aren't aching, though. They're not even chapped." He ducked beneath the covers before Lorcan could stop him. Enveloped in warmth and the scent of Lorcan's body, he licked Lorcan's shaft from root to tip, savoring the salty flavor. The light changed and he realized that Lorcan had thrown the sheets back, uncovering him. Rowan stilled as Lorcan wound fingers into his hair holding him in place.

"Do I need to remind you who's in charge here?" Lorcan's stern tone was edged with amusement.

"No, Sir." Rowan peeked at Lorcan's face to find him grinning.

"Is your inner brat coming to the surface?"

Rowan responded to a sharp tug on his hair with a moan. He loved it when Lorcan played with his hair. He shook his head.

"I like your spirit, Rowan. I don't think there's a brattish bone in your body. When you serve, when you submit to me, you glow. You seem utterly at peace in your submission. If only I could be the same in my dominance."

Rowan crawled up Lorcan's body, wrapping him in a hug. He guessed it was a rare event for Lorcan to show vulnerability and the moment touched Rowan deeply. He snuggled close while Lorcan ran his fingers through his hair, teasing out the tangles.

"I can't believe I stopped a blow job to get deep and meaningful," Lorcan muttered. "What an idiot."

"Not stopped, just delayed." That was an absolute certainty in Rowan's mind.

"Good to know."

"I suppose it's not my place to say, but I think you're a wonderful Dominant. I'm so lucky that you are the first person I get to look after here. You've spoiled me for anyone else. You make me feel…safe. Cherished. Even though this is only a temporary relationship, it's special to me. You push me to explore my boundaries but never pressure me. You take care of me after every scene. But best of all, you have this amazing aura of control — like nothing will happen unless you command it. I love that."

"What if this arrangement didn't have to be temporary?"

Rowan froze, hope blossoming in his heart. "I don't understand. What do you mean?"

"This place is a suspension of reality and soon I'll have to leave. I'm not sure I want to do that without you."

Rowan held his breath, until Lorcan gave his arse a squeeze, reminding him of the need for oxygen.

"Take deep breaths, Rowan. I don't want you passing out on me. At least not unless it's the result of me fucking you into oblivion."

"I think since the first day we met I've been hoping that our time together wouldn't have to end. When you told me you were planning to live in the UK, I thought that maybe you might want to see me again, but it was just a dream."

"I went to London yesterday to talk to some people about setting up a charitable foundation. I have a lot of money, Rowan. More than I could ever use in several extravagant lifetimes. My needs are simple—and I don't mean that I want to be destitute. I enjoy my comforts and I've worked hard to be in a position where I'm able to indulge myself, but I want my money to do some good, and I want to be personally involved. I'm going to need help with that from an assistant who understands me."

"You mean, you want me to work for you?"

"I think any contract of employment might be a little more extensive than is usual for a personal assistant."

"I don't know what to say." Rowan's thoughts were in a whirl.

"Then don't say anything. Put that pretty mouth to work elsewhere."

"Is that an order, Sir?"

"Yeah, it is."

Rowan kissed his way down Lorcan's body to find his cock had softened. It didn't take him long to tease it back to life with gentle licks and nibbles. He took Lorcan's shaft deep into his throat, swallowing around the obstruction. The knowledge Lorcan controlled his very breath sent shivers of pleasure through him. He pulled back, sucking as he went. He took his time, wanting to tease out Lorcan's pleasure. A slight tremor betrayed the moment when Lorcan's orgasm began. Warm seed gushed into Rowan's mouth and he swallowed, trying to capture every drop. Beneath him, Lorcan shuddered.

"Remind me to write blow jobs into the contract."

"Yes, Sir." Rowan kept a straight face, but inside he was laughing. A knock at the door told him that breakfast had arrived. He slipped out of bed to let Benjy in. He was pushing a trolley loaded with food and Rowan's stomach rumbled. Benjy grinned and Rowan realized he was standing there, stark naked, rigid erection bouncing. He sighed. No doubt his state would be the talk of the kitchen the rest of the day. He shrugged, far too happy to care. A whole new world of possibilities had opened up and he couldn't wait to explore what that might mean.

Chapter Eleven

"I'm so hyped." Rowan bounced from one side of the entrance hall to the other, straightening pictures and adjusting ornaments that didn't need to be moved. He only slowed down after banging his knee on the corner of an Elizabethan linen chest, which proved to be a lot sturdier than his tender flesh.

"You should be exhausted after the last few days," Rayne said. "I feel like I earned my money with the amount of driving I've done and I didn't have to hike round all those big houses."

Rowan rubbed his knee. "But it was wonderful. I got to see properties I'd never normally set foot in. Mr. Wilder seemed to like the ones I picked out and the pub lunches were fun—I think he's addicted to scampi and chips. Don't tell Tor."

"Where is the big bad Dom, anyway? I just want to check if he needs me tomorrow."

"He's in the office with Mr. Redding. He said he wouldn't be long. We don't have any more appointments set up until we go to London next week so if you like, I can ask him then let you know later."

"Okay, sounds good. After all the canoodling you two did in the back of the car, I have to go clean the leather upholstery."

"Canoodle? Were you born in the Victorian era? Who uses words like that?"

"My gran does." Rayne grinned. "She'd even scare the pants off Mr. Wilder."

"Hey! Nobody sees him with his pants off except me!"

"Who's taking their pants off?" Lorcan appeared from Luke's office. Rayne scuttled for the door. "Is our chauffeur making improper suggestions to you? I'm sure I could persuade Mr. Redding to give him a well-deserved whipping."

"I wouldn't take much persuading," Luke shouted from inside his office. "He's well overdue some discipline."

Rowan giggled. "He was telling me about his gran, Sir. Are you planning on going out tomorrow? I promised to let him know."

"After the last few days, I think we deserve some quiet time here. I've been neglecting your needs."

"You'd never neglect me, Sir."

"Go on, go after him."

Rowan dashed to the door, calling after Rayne to let him know that he could relax and clean the car at his leisure. He turned to find Lorcan staring at him, hands on his hips.

"You're like a kid on a sugar high," he said.

Rowan went to his knees in front of him.

"I'm sorry, Sir. The last few days have been so much fun but I have all this information jostling for space in my head. It's hard to calm down and think. The places we visited were all so grand, it was a glimpse into another world and I think I'm a bit scared of it all." He was talking too much and subsided into silence.

"Go on."

Rowan raised his eyes. Lorcan seemed genuinely interested.

"Working at the hotel, I got to meet lots of very wealthy people. A few were awful, some were perfectly nice. But… They never saw me as a person. I was there to provide a service and they never looked past that. I'm not saying they should have. Good service should be invisible. But it felt like there was a barrier, unspoken, unseen but impenetrable between their world and mine. Viewing those houses over the last few days felt like sneaking out of bounds. It was exciting, but not quite real."

"You would bring grace and care to any of those grand houses," Lorcan said. "The question is not whether you are worthy of them but whether they deserve you. Whether I deserve you."

He took Rowan's hand, bringing him to his feet. "Let's go and persuade Tor and his minions to rustle up a late afternoon tea for us. I think we will forgo dinner so that I can spend some time calming you down. So point me in the direction of the kitchen, it's about time I put in a personal appearance."

When they reached the kitchen, they found Tor delivering a lesson to Benjy and Frank. Rowan wasn't sure what he was teaching them, but the smells emanating from the stove were delicious. Tor caught sight of him hovering in the doorway, then spotted Lorcan. He wiped his hands on a cloth before strolling across to them.

"Good afternoon, Mr. Wilder. Have you come for a cooking lesson?"

"I'd much rather eat the food you and the boys prepare," Lorcan said. "I'm afraid I've been known to burn water."

Benjy and Frank both giggled until Tor glared at them and they both found interesting things to stare at on the floor.

"If it's not inconvenient, would you be able to manage a few sandwiches and a slice of cake? I have a hankering for an English afternoon tea, but we can wait if you're in the middle of something," Lorcan said.

"Not at all. In fact, your timing is perfect. I've been teaching the boys how to make Cullen skink and it needs to simmer for a while, so we can take a break. Where would you like to eat?"

"If we eat in the breakroom, Tor and the boys could join us. It would be fun," Rowan whispered in Lorcan's ear.

"If it's okay with you, Tor, Rowan has suggested we eat here, together. An afternoon tea party, if you like."

Tor chuckled. "You might live to regret this. When these three get together, they are just going to gossip about us."

"I'll risk it. It's good for Rowan to have company other than me and we haven't had the chance to talk very much yet either."

"In that case, go on through to the breakroom. The boys both made cakes this morning, practicing some new recipes, so you and Rowan can be our guinea pigs. I'll whip up some sandwiches and be right through. Frank, make a pot of tea. Benjy, set the table."

Rowan took Lorcan through to the breakroom while a scurry of activity kicked off in the kitchen.

"Thank you for doing this." He eyed the hard floor, wondering if Lorcan would want him to kneel.

"Sit at the table, Rowan. I know you want to talk to your friends and you can't do that if you're kneeling next to me. There will be plenty of time for you to get on your knees later, I promise." He winked, and Rowan's face warmed as he caught the meaning behind Lorcan's words.

Relieved, Rowan took a seat on one side of the table. It wasn't long before the others joined them in a clatter of crockery and excited chatter. Tor produced smoked salmon sandwiches and a plate of cheese scones, still warm from the oven. Rowan's mouth watered and it only got worse when Frank and Benjy brought through the cakes they had baked.

Rowan chatted to Frank and Benjy, describing his house-hunting adventures, while Lorcan spoke quietly with Tor. Every now and again Rowan glanced Lorcan's way, checking that he was enjoying himself. He seemed quite content.

After consuming several sandwiches and a scone, there was no way Rowan could choose between Frank's chocolate creation and Benjy's layered lemon fondant sponge. He ended up having a piece of each, as did Lorcan. Tor excused his double helping as a taste test and it was fun to watch Benjy and Frank on the edge of their seats as they awaited his verdict.

"Both excellent," Tor declared. "I'll make decent chefs out of the pair of you yet."

"What about you, Mr. Wilder? Do you have a favorite?" Benjy asked, batting his lashes.

Rowan laughed at his shameless antics.

"I couldn't possibly choose between them." Lorcan mouthed 'help me' at Rowan.

"I loved them both too," Rowan said. "But I think I need a nap. All this wonderful food has made me drowsy." He leaned toward Lorcan, whose eyes flashed.

"Time to leave, I think. Thank you, Tor, for the wonderful meal. I won't require dinner tonight."

Tor gave him a conspiratorial smile. "Just call if you need a late-night snack. Benjy is on duty this evening and will be glad to help."

Lorcan put his arm around Rowan's shoulders and guided him from the room.

"Thank you! My diplomatic skills were about to be tested to the limit."

"I imagine Tor will analyze both those cakes within an inch of their lives now we're gone. He's a perfectionist and a great teacher."

"And now you have sugar inside you, you're even more in need of some calm. With all the visiting we've been doing, I've not been taking care of you properly."

"Is there time for me to go take a shower, Sir?"

"Sure. It'll give me a chance to prepare. You have an hour to get ready for me. Come to the Blue Room and wear something I'll appreciate."

"Yes, Sir. Did you have anything specific in mind?"

"Less than you're wearing now. Exactly what that is, I'll leave to you. Surprise me. You now have fifty-nine minutes."

Rowan ran to his room, eager to prepare. Visiting properties in the Cotswolds had been fun but he was ready for some one-on-one attention from his Dom.

* * * *

Lorcan glanced at his watch. There were still ten minutes until Rowan was due to return and Lorcan was getting impatient. A quick call to Luke Redding had secured a collection of fat pillar candles that now glimmered around the room. Luke had also agreed to the temporary disabling of the room's smoke detector on the understanding that Lorcan would be flayed alive if he didn't re-arm it the instant the scene was done. Lorcan had showered then changed into an outfit that he knew would make Rowan's cock stand to attention. Supple leather pants hung so low on his hips that if he bent over, his ass would be on display. He'd opted to forgo a shirt in favor of a black suede vest, or waistcoat as Rowan would call it. He'd debated over boots but decided to go barefoot because what he had planned involved climbing on the bed. Checking the equipment he'd selected, Lorcan was surprised at how nervous he felt. Since he'd suggested to Rowan that their relationship might continue, his feelings had deepened, bringing new emotions into play whenever they were together.

Over the last few days he'd seen a different side to Rowan, who had revealed himself to be an intelligent, perceptive young man, full of curiosity and questions. Protecting him from the harsh world Lorcan knew had become paramount. Lorcan didn't want anything to affect Rowan's innocent enthusiasm. He felt the weight of responsibility for keeping Rowan safe and providing for his needs as a man as well as a submissive. Rowan hadn't yet given him a definitive answer as to whether he would leave The Retreat to become Lorcan's assistant and Lorcan had noticed glimmers of doubt in his eyes. He guessed he was conflicted about letting Carey Hoffman down and nervous about stepping into the unknown with a man he'd only met a few weeks before. It was a huge step to take and Lorcan wished he could give Rowan more time to make his decision, but he only had a few days left of his stay and didn't want to leave without him. He'd just have to give him all the reassurance he could. Rowan had to make his own choice in his own time, and Lorcan hoped that the scene he had planned for the evening would help clear Rowan's mind.

He fingered the complex arrangement of leather straps lying across the bed where he had lowered the sling usually concealed in the bed's canopy. Once Rowan was safely restrained there was a mechanism that would automatically raise him above the mattress. Lorcan would have access to his body from both sides and one end. He planned to arrange him in a way that gave him a sense of weightlessness in suspension. If he could make Rowan focus on his body rather than the jumble of thoughts in his head, it might calm his worries and help him decide his future. Of course, it would also give Lorcan the satisfaction of having complete control and the gift of Rowan's trust. He'd put on a cock ring because the preparations alone had made him hard. He wanted to be able to concentrate on coaxing Rowan to fly rather than his own basic urges.

A soft tap at the door told him that Rowan had finally arrived. Lorcan opened it to let him in, eager to see his reaction to the candlelit room. Rowan's eyes widened as he took in the scene. Lorcan imagined his own expression wasn't that different when he saw what Rowan was wearing. The sheer white silk thong barely covered his package, the fabric so flimsy the slightest tug would rip it free. Lorcan resolved to do just that as soon as he had Rowan where he wanted him.

"This is beautiful, Sir. I love candlelight."

Rowan sank to his knees. He clasped his hands behind his back and lowered his head. Lorcan took a few deep breaths. Part of him wanted to take Rowan right there on the floor. He was temptation packaged in blond hair, blue eyes and a sleek body. But a quick fuck wasn't what Rowan needed right then and every overprotective bone in Lorcan's body vibrated with the need to take care of him.

"This evening I'm going to clear your mind of all the noise. You don't have to think about anything except the pleasure you give me through your submission." He brushed Rowan's cheek with the back of one finger, eliciting a sweet whimper. "You can stand." Rowan came to his feet, eyes still downcast. Lorcan indulged himself by stroking smooth, warm skin. He pulled Rowan's thong down to rest beneath his balls, displaying them and his stiff cock.

"So hard for me." He took Rowan's shaft in a loose grip. Heat soaked into his palm. "You don't have permission to come. I'll let you know when it pleases me to give you release."

"Yes, Sir," Rowan whispered.

Lorcan stepped away. "I want you to lie on the bed. Have you ever used a sling before?"

Rowan shook his head. "I've seen one used a few times, but I've never been in one myself." He levered himself onto the bed, wriggling into position so that the largest section of leather lay beneath his back and shoulders.

"I'm going to blindfold you. I want your senses focused on my touch and being deprived of sight will help. I'm not going to use earplugs because it's quiet enough in here and I'm selfish enough to want to hear the sounds you make, so no gag." Lorcan adjusted the positions of some of the straps. "I'm not going to talk very much but I'll be here. I won't leave you."

Rowan blinked, his eyes huge. "I trust you, Sir."

Lorcan's throat tightened and he had to turn away. He fetched the blindfold, fastening it around Rowan's head. Covering Rowan's eyes helped Lorcan concentrate, something he found hard to do when Rowan's gaze sliced through every layer of his emotional armor. He spent the next ten minutes securing Rowan's limbs in straps designed to support his weight and reduce the strain on his muscles. He checked every fastening carefully to ensure that nothing would pinch or rub. The sling was designed in such a way that Rowan's legs would be held apart, but bent at the knees. His arms would rest at his sides, strapped close so that he would not be able to move them. Supports beneath his neck and head would ensure he couldn't hurt himself if he thrashed around.

Lorcan made sure to touch Rowan often, reassuring him of his presence. When he pressed the button to start the automatic lift, he didn't give Rowan any warning. He didn't want to raise him too far, just enough that he would feel weightless. He locked the hoist when Rowan was around eighteen inches above the mattress then moved around him, checking all the straps again. Rowan's breathing, which had initially sped up, calmed. He gave a soft sigh.

Lorcan knew that whatever happened between them in the future, he would remember this moment always. Rowan's absolute trust that Lorcan would take care of him, his utter faith that he wouldn't be hurt, brought tears to Lorcan's eyes. He rubbed the back of his hand across them, brushing away the moisture. He hadn't cried in many years, maintaining rigid control over his emotions. Rowan had turned Lorcan's world inside out by handing him power over his body, though he knew only too well that it was really Rowan who had the power over him.

He put a leather strap around the base of Rowan's balls, cinching it tight, then tore the skimpy thong from his body. He fondled Rowan's cock until he moaned.

"That's it, boy. Let go."

Lorcan slipped his hand into a soft, fur glove. He stroked Rowan's body from shoulder to thigh, then across his abs to brush his nipples. Rowan shivered, humming his pleasure. Lorcan kept the pressure light but continuous, touching every part of Rowan's frame but avoiding his cock. When all traces of tension had disappeared from Rowan's muscles, Lorcan swapped the glove for a Wartenberg wheel. He pressed it into his palm to judge how much pressure he should use, surprised at the sting. He ran the instrument across the sole of Rowan's foot. Rowan's entire body jerked in his restraints, setting the sling in motion. Lorcan smiled and continued to run the vicious tool across Rowan's skin, leaving a trail of tiny red dots in its wake. When Lorcan tracked the wheel across his nipples a few times, Rowan's breath sped up and his hands clenched into fists. Lorcan pressed a little harder, though not enough to break skin, taking the wheel close to Rowan's groin before tracking down the inside of his thigh.

It was time to swap toys again so Lorcan exchanged the pinwheel for a length of silk. He dragged it across Rowan's belly then let it drift over his erection, ghosting over the head of his dick. Rowan strained against the straps holding him in place as if the touch of silk was more painful than the metal spikes which had preceded it. Lorcan looped the silk around Rowan's cock, tying it loosely so that he could brush it up and down and provide more friction.

"Please…"

"Something to say, Rowan?"

"I…"

"I didn't think so."

Lorcan exchanged the silk for a candle with liquid wax pooled in the well around its wick. He blew out the flame then, holding the candle high enough above Rowan's body that the wax would cool on its descent, he allowed two drops to fall on Rowan's belly where they immediately solidified into flat white discs. Rowan yelped, yanking hard on his wrist restraints. Lorcan trailed drops of wax up his abdomen, letting the final two splash on each nipple in turn. This time Rowan screamed.

Lorcan put the candle back, re-lighting it with a match, knowing that Rowan would hear the scrape.

"Don't want to run out of wax, do we?" Lorcan grinned. Even though Rowan couldn't see him, he would detect the mischief in his voice.

"You're very cruel, Sir." Rowan didn't sound unhappy about it.

"I can be." Lorcan fetched the ice bucket, placing it on the bed within easy reach. Using his nail, he lifted the wax discs adhered to Rowan's skin, then he took an ice cube and rubbed it over the red patches. Rowan gasped, but soon settled. Lorcan repeated the process for each piece of wax, leaving Rowan's nipples until last. He applied ice to both sides at the same time, soothing the small hurts he had created. Rowan wriggled as much as he was able until Lorcan stilled the sling. He ran a cube of ice from Rowan's chest across his stomach, following a pinwheel track to his groin where he let the remains of the ice melt. He wrapped his cold hand around Rowan's balls, giving them a gentle squeeze.

"Sir!"

"You're so hot in my hand. So eager. But you have to wait a while longer because I'm not done with you yet."

Rowan moaned, the sound sweet to Lorcan's ears. He took the ice away and dried his hands on a towel. His fingers were still chilled so when he pushed them inside his pants to caress his own aching cock, the cold was a shock. Just what he needed. He was glad Rowan wasn't able to see his expression because he was probably doing a fair impression of Munch's painting, *The Scream*. Once he'd recovered, he dried Rowan's skin with care then collected the vibrating plug he had chosen. It was thick and heavy, made from steel. He applied a layer of lube then pressed it to Rowan's grasping hole. It slid home easily, not big enough to cause Rowan any discomfort. Lorcan put the control on a low setting before turning it on. He could just hear a whirr as the toy vibrated inside Rowan's body. Rowan sank his teeth into his lower lip, bucking his hips.

"Keep it inside you," Lorcan ordered.

"I can't... It's too much, Sir."

"I don't hear your safe word, Rowan. Until I do, I decide what's too much." Lorcan turned the vibrator up a notch. "Or not enough." Lorcan watched for a minute while Rowan's entire body trembled. Mumbled, desperate words issued from plump, pink lips but they didn't make any sense. Lorcan smiled as he collected a violet wand from the dresser. It had been a while since he'd used one but when he plugged it in, the distinctive buzz was familiar. On its lowest setting, the jolt of electricity against his skin was little more than a pleasant vibration, set higher the spark of pain was more intense. Lorcan rubbed the spot where the tiny arc of lightning had hit his arm. In the candlelit room, the wand glowed and he debated removing Rowan's blindfold so that he could see what was happening. Deciding against it, Lorcan reset the wand to low. He brushed his fingers down Rowan's bare arm to let him know that he was close again. Rowan, completely absorbed by the sensation of the vibrator inside him, didn't react. He was close to letting go completely and that was Lorcan's ultimate goal.

Beginning with Rowan's shoulder, Lorcan moved the wand down his body in regular increments. It was a while before Rowan noticed what was happening but Lorcan detected a change in his breathing.

"What's that, Sir?"

"Electricity." He didn't enlighten Rowan further. Instead he turned up the setting and targeted Rowan's nipples, making him jerk.

"Hurts so good."

"It does. No more talking, just feel. Clear your mind."

The tiny crackles and flashes of light from the wand fascinated Lorcan, as did the way Rowan's muscles twitched at each contact. He worked his way lower, wanting Rowan to know exactly where he was heading. The first lightning bolt to Rowan's inner thigh made him wail and thrash. Lorcan used the wand again and again, not letting up. Putting the wand back on low, he removed Rowan's cock ring, then made one final contact with the tip of his cock. Rowan came, screaming Lorcan's name, cum splashing his belly. Lorcan unplugged the wand then stripped, removing his own cock ring. He knelt on the bed between

Rowan's legs. The sling suspended Rowan at the perfect height to take Lorcan's cock. He eased the vibrator from Rowan's body, replacing it immediately with his aching dick. Rowan's channel was slick and hot, gripping him, his inner muscles working him hard. Lorcan grabbed the straps of the sling that raised Rowan's legs, pulling them wider apart to give him better access. He used the movement of the sling to drive deeper into Rowan's body. The position wasn't the easiest but the rewards were worth it. He came far too soon, the brief moment of ecstasy blanking his senses. He thrust a few more times, riding the wave of orgasm until his thighs trembled and he slipped from Rowan's body. Maintaining the presence of mind to lower the sling safely and disconnect it from the bed took iron willpower. Rowan was limp and pliant, semiconscious. Once he was able to slide the mess of leather from beneath Rowan's body, Lorcan dumped it on the floor. He slumped on the bed next to Rowan, pulling him close. He stroked his skin and whispered nonsense to him that Rowan probably couldn't hear. He was floating, his expression serene. Tired, but still experiencing the rush of adrenaline, Lorcan watched candle flames flicker. He didn't want to sleep just yet. Listening to Rowan's breathing was enough.

Chapter Twelve

Rowan's wonderful dream was disturbed when Lorcan began to mumble in his sleep. Rowan turned onto his side so that he could see Lorcan's face. The curtains weren't quite drawn and the silver light of dawn seeped into the room, casting the bed in shadows. Lorcan frowned, his forehead creased. Rowan put a hand on his shoulder, which usually helped calm him but this time it had no effect. Lorcan's voice got louder and he began to pull at the covers as if he felt trapped. He repeated the word 'no' over and over again, his voice becoming more strident. Suddenly, he sat bolt upright, eyes open. For a moment Rowan thought he might still be asleep then he gave a shuddering sigh and turned to face him.

"I'm sorry. I woke you."

"It doesn't matter," Rowan said. "I don't want to waste a minute of the day."

Lorcan pulled him into a hug. "How do you feel this morning?"

"Good. Relaxed, Sir. Last night was amazing. I felt like I was floating and that everything I'd been worried about disappeared. There was just you, me and sensations I never knew my body could experience." He sighed. "I hope I can persuade you to use the sling again before you have to leave." He couldn't quite bring himself to say before *we* have to leave. He'd made up his mind, but needed to talk to a few people first. If Lorcan noticed the particular use of words, he didn't comment.

"I think I'm going to head to the gym for an early work out. Why don't you come with me?"

"I'd love to swim, Sir. It might stretch out my muscles a bit."

"Something I'd enjoy seeing." Lorcan leered.

"I don't have any clothes here." Rowan batted his lashes. "I vaguely recall someone ripping my underwear off last night."

"That might have happened, but I'm admitting to nothing. Besides, you don't need clothes to swim."

Rowan giggled. He'd happily run around naked all day if it took Lorcan's mind from whatever was tormenting him.

Two hours later, he wasn't feeling quite so magnanimous. Lorcan had tied him to a bench in the gym before delivering his morning discipline. He'd then made him sit on his sore behind while he'd pounded out the miles on the treadmill and, though the view had been good, it hadn't made up for the pain when Rowan had stood, peeling his arse from the vinyl. The cold water of the pool had been wonderful but watching Lorcan swim naked had kept him so hard it impeded his ability to move around. Then Lorcan had taken him back to the Blue Room and watched from a chair while Rowan jacked himself off. His cock was now imprisoned in a steel cage, much heavier than the acrylic chastity device Lorcan had used before. He was also plugged, and both the cage and the plug were held in place by a leather belt buckled around his hips with a strap that nestled between his arse cheeks, divided either side of his balls and fastened at the front of the belt, where it was locked in place. The acrylic device he'd been able to ignore, to some extent. This was impossible to forget. No doubt exactly what Lorcan intended.

As he knelt next to Lorcan's chair at the breakfast table in the snug, Rowan was grateful for the cushion beneath his knees. He could still taste the bacon Lorcan had fed him, the salt lingering on his lips.

"Have you had enough to eat?" Lorcan asked.

"Yes, thank you, Sir. The bacon was delicious. You have it much crispier that it's usually served here and I prefer it."

"Bacon needs a crunch."

Lorcan sipped his coffee, his glance straying toward his phone, which lay on the table next to him. "I've been avoiding this for three weeks, but I need to check my messages. I'm kind of dreading what I might find."

Rowan rested his head against Lorcan's thigh, hoping that he might reveal a bit more of himself.

"I left San Francisco without saying goodbye to anyone, except my best friend Giles. I wanted a clean break from the business and the people involved with it. The constant questions about my plans were driving me mad but I'm not the kind of person that can sit idle." His fingers strayed toward the phone.

"If you don't mind me saying, Sir, if you think the time is right to reconnect then it probably is."

"Gut instinct, you mean?"

"Perhaps."

"It can't have escaped your notice, Rowan, that I prefer to be in control of all aspects of my life."

Rowan gave his imprisoned cock a wry glance. "Yes, Sir, I had noticed."

"Sarcasm will get you a spanking." Lorcan chuckled. "Of course, you will enjoy that as much as I will. It's a far preferable activity to looking at this." He tapped the phone. "However, it's time." He switched it on and, once everything had loaded, glanced at the screen. "Holy crap. I didn't realize I was so popular." He held the phone up so that Rowan could see the screen.

"Wow... That's a lot. I get one or two voicemails a day at most. You have hundreds and thousands of emails."

Lorcan sighed. "Is your computer still set up in the banqueting hall?"

"Yes, Sir."

"In that case, today you are a personal assistant as well as my submissive. We have work to do. Of course, that's if I can concentrate at all with you dressed like that."

"I could put some clothes on, Sir."

"No. Absolutely not. I have to get some pleasure out of the day." Lorcan chuckled. "I wonder what my previous assistant would have thought if I'd ordered him to work naked."

Rowan giggled. "I don't imagine it was in his job description, Sir."

"Perhaps it should have been. It will be in yours, if you decide to come with me at the end of the week and no, I'm not asking for an answer now." Lorcan poured himself a fresh cup of coffee. "Go and check that everything we'll need is in the banqueting hall. Make sure it's nice and warm in there. Then let the kitchen know that we'll have a working lunch in there too. I want to get through this lot today so we can enjoy the rest of the week."

Getting to his feet, Rowan winced. He was a little sore.

"Do you need the plug removed?" Lorcan asked, resting a hand on Rowan's hip.

"That's not the bit of me that's sore, Sir. My shoulders ache a bit — from the sling, I think."

"I should have given you better aftercare last night." Lorcan stood. He massaged Rowan's shoulders, his touch soothing.

"Given that I don't remember much about it, Sir, I don't think there's a lot you could have done. I had a wonderful time and this is nothing serious. The stiffness will be gone in a day or two, I'm sure."

"Other parts of you won't be getting stiff for a while." He gave Rowan's arse a pat then tapped the steel cage around his cock.

"No, Sir. Will chastity be a part of the role description too?"

"Oh, definitely."

"Then I'll need to consider my options very carefully."

"Brat. Get going, before I bend you over my knee."

Rowan didn't think that was much of an incentive to move.

* * * *

"God damn it! This is why I sold the business in the first place." Lorcan shoved his chair back from the banqueting table to pace the room. "These people think they have the right to every detail of my life." The stress he'd left behind in the U.S. threatened to ruin his day until he caught sight of Rowan wriggling on his chair. His cheeks were flushed, his hair tousled where he kept running his fingers through it. When he caught sight of Lorcan staring, he stilled.

"I forwarded my messages to Giles while I traveled," Lorcan explained. "Then took off the redirect when I arrived. He has enough to deal with. Then I turned off the phone and it has been bliss."

"And it will be again, Sir. I've deleted all the spam and sorted the rest of the email into personal, business and not sure. That's just going on the subject lines, so I might have a few wrong. You'll need to listen to the voicemails, but that won't take long."

"Fine." Lorcan knew he sounded like a petulant teenager but he didn't care. "I'll do that now." He gave each call exactly five seconds before deleting it if it had anything to do with his old business. Two calls from his parents were just them checking in with no real expectation of a response. "Make a list, Rowan. One— call my parents."

Rowan tapped away on the keyboard.

"Two—get a new phone number."

Giggling, Rowan added that to the list.

Lorcan listened to a few more messages. Ninety-five percent of the callers wanted something from him. There were a couple of thank yous from charities he had supported and he got Rowan to add them to the list so that he could do a bit of research into them. "I want you to know the kind of causes I'm interested in," he explained. "I like to know where my money is going and I'll expect you to make recommendations based on sound evidence."

"I'm sorry, Sir... I don't understand." Rowan blinked. *God, he has the most beautiful, distracting eyes.* Lorcan realized he was staring. Rowan must think he was crazy.

"One of my assistant's responsibilities is to screen my calls and email. I intend to set up a charitable foundation and there will be an application process for organizations seeking grants. The initial research is important because I'll have limited time to do more in-depth investigation and I will want to limit that to causes with a realistic chance of being accepted. That means careful, meticulous, initial desk research, clear reports and recommendations. I'm being presumptuous, I know. But I'd like you to know the kind of things you'd be expected to do if you decide to work for me. Unfortunately, I can't spend twenty-four hours a day in the nearest dungeon, enticing though that idea is." That put another idea in his head. "Something else for your list. See if you can find some craftsmen who make high-quality dungeon furniture. Once I've decided on a property, creating a state-of-the-art playroom will be top of my priority list. Carey Hoffman or someone else at The Underground will be able to give you some ideas, I'm sure. I've also heard on the grapevine about a carpenter working in Cornwall who creates unique pieces."

"I'm sure I can find him online, Sir. And there is some amazing equipment at the club. I went there once for an open day." Rowan shifted on his chair.

"I've been a member for several years," Lorcan said. "But I only ever got to London once or twice a year so I haven't been that often. That's something else I want to change about my life."

"Did you always know you were a Dominant, Sir?" Rowan asked. "I'm sorry, I shouldn't be asking personal questions." He rocked a little.

"You realize that by moving around, you are just tormenting yourself." With Rowan's cock encased in metal, Lorcan imagined the plug must be administering a unique form of torture, especially if it was pressing against Rowan's prostate. "And I don't mind you asking me questions, though I can't guarantee I'll always answer them. Some things are best left in the past."

To his credit, Rowan didn't allow his curiosity to get the better of him. He remained silent. Lorcan rested his backside on the table next to him. He was a bit conflicted as to whether he should tell Rowan anything, but decided it couldn't hurt to share a little bit about himself. If he wanted Rowan to take a leap of faith then he owed it to him to do the same.

"I suppose I knew I wanted to be in charge from an early age. Not that I recognized it as dominance at the time, but all through high school I had brushes with authority. Not because I wanted to make trouble but because I didn't like having other people in control of my life. My parents always told me I was too intelligent for my own good. I got bored easily. Rules and regulations were fine as long as I was the one setting them." He glanced at Rowan, taking in his near nudity, the leather around his hips and the metal encasing his cock. Rowan's condition was at his command and it gave him no end of pleasure. He brushed Rowan's bare shoulder with the backs of his fingers. "Something happened that made me doubt what I wanted, what I needed. You don't need to know the details, but it took me a long time and years of therapy to come to terms with my nature. I hid behind my work, only venturing into the world of Domination and submission on rare occasions. Then, a couple of years ago, the iron grip I had on my life started to slip. I thought more and more about how short life is and how we shouldn't waste what little time we have. I didn't want to reach my thirties full of regrets so I decided to take the steps needed to get the kind of life I really wanted. Accepting my Dominant side was a catalyst for change. It took two years to plan how I would divest myself of the things that stopped me living life my way. Selling a multibillion dollar business is not straightforward."

"I can't tell you how much I admire what you've done, Sir." A delicate blush rose on Rowan's cheeks.

"But you've done the same," Lorcan said. "You could have stayed in your old job, safe and secure, but you took the brave step to come here because a life of submission called to you."

"It's hardly the same thing, Sir," Rowan protested.

"The scale may be different, but I think we are more similar than you might like to admit."

Rowan shook his head. "I like to look after people and I like to be told what to do, that's all."

"It's a good job I like ordering you around then, isn't it?" Lorcan didn't push him any further. "I hid behind my work, you hid in a country hotel but now there's no more hiding for either of us. What do you look for in a good Dominant, Rowan?"

Rowan stared at his computer screen for a full minute without speaking. Lorcan held his tongue, resisting the urge to break the silence.

"Someone who is firm, but kind. Someone who sees what I can't articulate, sees me, knows what I need even when I don't. A man who appreciates being served and doesn't take advantage. Someone who is comfortable in his skin and can make me feel the same in mine."

"You have high standards, Rowan."

"I'm handing over control of my body and to a certain extent my mind. That kind of trust has to be earned."

"I agree." Lorcan wondered if he was anywhere close to being what Rowan needed. A rare moment of uncertainty struck him. He covered his unease by listening to some more messages.

"Hmm. That's a surprise. My friend Giles is going to be in London tonight for a brief visit. He and his father are on their way to Amsterdam on business. He's asked if I want to come and meet them for dinner." He checked his watch. There was still plenty of time to get to the city.

"Rowan, could you please go and ask Mr. Redding if Rayne is free to drive me. He'll need to stay late to bring me back."

Rowan got up and made his way to the door. Lorcan kept track of every step, every movement of Rowan's buttocks as he walked, the flex of each muscle. He shook his head. Rowan captivated him. He was torn between not wanting to leave him behind and not being ready to share him, even with Giles. It could be a moot point if Rayne wasn't available. He should have checked his messages sooner.

Rowan was gone no more than a minute or two.

"It's fine, Sir. Mr. Redding sent Rayne into town this morning, but he's back so it's no problem for you to use the car. Rayne will wait in London while you have dinner."

"I'll text Giles now to let him know I'm on my way. He and his father are staying at the Ritz. I...don't want to share you, Rowan."

"I understand, Sir. There's plenty for me to do here."

"Let's go upstairs. You can help me get ready then have the rest of the afternoon off while I'm away. You've had hardly any time to yourself since I arrived and it only seems fair that if I'm off enjoying myself, you should too." He took Rowan's hand, brushing his thumb across the smooth palm as they walked to the stairs.

"What will you do, while I'm gone?"

"I think I'll have a long soak in the bath with lots of bubbles and my book. I'll call my aunt and Ed then spend some time recovering from the ear bashing they're both likely to give me. They are both way too interested in my life and want to know every detail of what goes on here. They know I can't tell them but they keep asking anyway." He laughed. "I'll miss you."

"Don't worry, I'm going to give you something to remember me by while I'm gone." Lorcan pushed open the door to the Blue Room. "Hands and knees on the bed."

"Yes, Sir." Rowan scrambled into position.

Lorcan went straight to the toy chest. He selected a rectangular paddle, its rubber-coated surface covered in dimples. He swiped it through the air a couple of times, flexing his wrist. The weight felt good in his hand. Four sharp blows, two to each cheek, and Rowan's ass glowed pink.

"Now you'll be reminded of me every time you sit down," Lorcan said, satisfied with his work.

"Thank you, Sir." Rowan's tone was wry. He collapsed onto his belly, face buried in the pillow.

"Turn over." Once Rowan had executed an uncoordinated roll, Lorcan inserted the key to the padlock holding his belt closed. He removed it, and the plug, with care. "Much as I would like to leave you stuffed full for the rest of the day, I don't know what time I'll be back." He gave Rowan's metal-encased cock a pat. "I want you to sleep in this bed tonight. Don't wait up for me. Just be here."

"Yes, Sir."

Rowan's shy smile melted Lorcan's heart. He almost changed his mind about going into London but decided that it would be good for Rowan to have some time to himself. He needed to think through his options without the pressure of Lorcan's presence.

Once he was primped and dressed, Lorcan gave Rowan a chaste kiss goodbye before heading down to the main hall. The front door stood open, letting in a mild breeze and Lorcan could see Rayne leaning on the car, waiting for him. He didn't go outside straightaway however but tapped on Luke Redding's office door.

"Come in."

Lorcan wondered if Luke ever relaxed. He always seemed to be working.

"Luke, do you have a moment?"

"Sure. Come in and take a seat. There's no problem, I hope?"

"With my stay, not at all," Lorcan reassured him. "Everything here has more than exceeded my expectations. This place really lives up to its name." He hesitated, uncertain how to put his next words.

"I sense a but." Luke smiled. "And, if I haven't completely lost my intuition, I'd guess it has something to do with young Rowan."

Lorcan stretched his legs, crossing his ankles in a semblance of relaxation he didn't feel.

"I've asked him to come with me when I leave." He held Luke's gaze.

"Do you mind if I ask in what capacity?" There was no challenge in Luke's tone, no aggression.

"As my assistant and my submissive." Saying it just reconfirmed to Lorcan that it was what he wanted. More than anything. "He's scared."

Luke steepled his fingers. "He worships you. Of course he is."

"He…wait… What?" Lorcan wasn't sure he'd heard Luke correctly.

"You're not just a job to him. That's blatantly obvious to everyone here. He's in love with you, Lorcan."

"But…"

"I'd guess he doesn't know that what he's feeling is love. He's young and you've rocked his world."

"He's only known me a few weeks."

"A few very intense weeks. You have to remember that Rowan gave up his old life to move here. He wanted it badly and now you're asking him to make another huge change. His emotions must be scrambled."

"I should stay here tonight."

"No, I don't think so. Some time alone will be good for him…and I have an idea."

"Care to fill me in?"

"Not yet. I need to make a call first but I will say this — Rowan was made to serve one man. Whether you deserve to be that man is yet to be proven…and that's not an insult, by the way. You need to prove it to yourself, not just to him."

Lorcan closed his eyes. "You are one hell of a scary guy, Luke."

"I try."

Lorcan opened one eye to find Luke grinning.

"You need a sub of your own. I'd bet good money you could tame the most incorrigible brat."

"It's true that no real Dominant is complete without a sub. The right man for me will come along one day. But we're not here to talk about me. Go to London. Enjoy yourself. I'll be here if Rowan needs me."

Lorcan drummed his fingers on his thigh. "Convenient way to change the subject, Luke. We should revisit this topic. Soon."

Luke could give the Mona Lisa a run for her money when it came to enigmatic smiles and Lorcan knew when he'd met his match. He pushed his chair back, feeling a bit like he'd been out-gunned. It was almost as if Luke had been expecting him, had known what he was going to talk about and had already considered every potential outcome. Lorcan guessed that The Retreat's manager was even more of a control freak than he was. He'd love to see him in action at The Underground, wielding a whip or a flogger. He imagined Luke would be able to deliver a masterclass in any and every form of domination.

"Have a good trip," Luke said. "Take care of Rayne."

Lorcan caught the smile that Luke tried to hide.

"I have earplugs, but don't worry, I'll keep an eye on the brat." Still a little reluctant to leave, Lorcan headed outside. It was a glorious afternoon and he sucked in a lung full of fresh air. Rayne waved, holding the car door open for him.

"It's a conspiracy," Lorcan muttered. "They can't wait to get me out of here." He shook his head. Perhaps a long conversation with Giles was what he needed. Some advice from a neutral party might help. "Boardroom negotiations were never this bad."

"Would it be disrespectful to point out that you're talking to yourself, Mr. Wilder?" Rayne affected wide-eyed innocence.

Lorcan sighed. It was going to be a long car ride to London.

Chapter Thirteen

It was a novelty for Rowan to have so much time to himself and he found he didn't like it. Without Lorcan he felt lost. He lay on the bed for a while, breathing in Lorcan's scent, but after a while he got fidgety. He spent some time cleaning and tidying the room, changing the bed and scrubbing the bathroom until it gleamed. When there was nothing left to do he took one of Lorcan's dress shirts from the wardrobe and shrugged it on. The tails just about covered his arse and would allow him a modicum of dignity while he walked back to his room. It was one thing to wander around naked when it was Lorcan's wish, but somehow felt entirely different without him.

He scuttled downstairs, managing to avoid getting any new bruises and keeping his fingers crossed that nobody would spot him. He made it as far as the banqueting hall where he caught sight of the computer. Before he even realized what he was doing he had taken the seat in front of it and turned it on. The pressure of the hard seat on his recently spanked behind made him think of Lorcan and he nibbled his lower lip, feeling guilty before he'd even done anything. He brought up the search engine, typed Lorcan's name into the box but hesitated, his finger hovering over the return key.

"Dammit." He stabbed the plastic. Millions of search results instantly flashed onto the screen. "In for a penny…"

Shoulders hunched, he leaned toward the screen, scanning the rows of text. Lorcan was famous. There were hundreds of articles about his business dealings, his charitable work and his associates. There were pictures of social events with him dressed in a dinner jacket and those made Rowan's mouth water and his cock twitch. But Rowan wasn't online to ogle pictures of the man he shared a bed with. The real thing was far more attractive. He dug deeper, going back in time to when Lorcan had started his business, and it was there he found a reference to something disturbing. He clicked on the link, which took him to a newspaper article giving an account of a violent home invasion.

Lorcan Wilder, 17, adopted son of Mr. and Mrs. Benjamin Wilder, was taken from the scene to the local hospital. There is no information at this time about his injuries. A police source informed journalists at the scene that Lorcan had been home alone at the time of the break-in. His parents are on their way back from a vacation in the Hamptons.

Rowan stopped reading and began to search for more information about the incident. It had been picked up by the national press and some of the more sensationalist periodicals and from a range of articles he managed to piece together what had happened.

Four men had broken into the property in the early hours of the morning. Lorcan had awoken and attempted to escape via a rear exit, having discovered that the phones had been disconnected. The gang had caught him then spent several hours assaulting him, before a concerned neighbor had reported the presence of a strange vehicle on the street. Hearing sirens, the men had made a run for it. Two of them had been arrested while the other two made their escape, but had later been tracked down. Lorcan had spent several weeks in hospital.

There was no information on what exactly had been done to him or what his specific injuries were and Rowan was relieved about that. His imagination was conjuring up quite enough horrors. He was convinced he had discovered the source of Lorcan's nightmares. He stared blindly at the computer screen, not sure what to do. He couldn't hide his knowledge from Lorcan but had no idea how he might react. Rowan powered down the computer and he was still sat with his fingers resting on the keyboard when Luke came into the room.

"Rowan? Are you okay? You're as pale as a ghost."

Rowan jumped at the sound of Luke's voice, then pasted a fake smile on his face. "I'm fine, thank you, Mr. Redding."

"You're not a good liar, Rowan." Luke went across to a sideboard and poured a tumbler of brandy from the decanter. He pressed the glass into Rowan's shaking hand. "Drink."

Rowan tossed back the golden liquid, which burned a trail down his throat into his stomach. He coughed, not used strong alcohol.

"I know you're worried about the future, Rowan. You need to do what's best for you. Mr. Wilder will respect that and I'll support you in whatever decision you make."

"It's not that, well, not just that. I shouldn't have been digging around, but I was interested. I wanted to know a bit more about him and he's not very forthcoming about his past. Something happened, a long time ago. I think it's the reason he has so many bad dreams."

"Mr. Hoffman does extensive and thorough background checks into everyone who applies to stay here. I know what you're talking about and I'm not surprised that the trauma has stayed with him, but it happened a long time ago and you shouldn't let what you know affect what you feel about him now. That wouldn't be fair."

"I'll have to tell him that I know," Rowan said. "He's going to be so angry."

"I think you should give him more credit." Luke squeezed Rowan's shoulder. "Go to your room, take a nap. Everything will seem better once you've rested. There's a lot going on in that pretty head of yours and you have some decisions to make. I know you find it hard without Mr. Wilder here, but these decisions have to be yours, Rowan, made without his influence. Come to dinner in the kitchen later. As Mr. Wilder is out it will be nice for us to get together."

"Okay." Rowan gave him a tentative smile. "That sounds good, and I am a little tired. I think I'll take a soak in the tub then snooze."

Luke nodded and strolled away in the direction of his office. Rowan unfolded himself from the uncomfortable chair then headed for his bedroom where he ran a bath, adding far too many bubbles. He had his choice of the same products used in the guest bedrooms and, as with everything at The Retreat, they were great quality. He put Lorcan's shirt on the back of a chair, grabbed his Kindle then clambered into the steaming water. As he lay back, he realized just how much tension had built in his neck and shoulders. The hot water soaked into his muscles and he moaned, relishing the deep heat treatment. He changed his mind about reading, put his Kindle on the floor, closed his eyes and tried to get his thoughts in order. He was distracted by the glint of metal beneath the water but realized that the chastity device meant that Lorcan was still with him, in a way.

Rowan wondered if that was how it would be if he decided to take Lorcan's job offer. The attraction of never being alone, never having to worry about making decisions by himself, was strong. Not that he didn't know his own mind, but Lorcan's presence always made him feel as if he was being looked after. He felt the same in bondage. Safe. Secure. Ropes and chains were just a replacement for Lorcan's arms.

His thoughts were invaded by visions of Lorcan as a young man and how terrified he must have been on that night all those years ago. Rowan couldn't bear to think what might have happened to him, been done to him, and he had no idea how he was going to raise the subject. Lorcan would know there was something on his mind. He had a way of looking into Rowan's soul and there was no hiding from his gaze. Rowan could be fully dressed yet stripped bare beneath Lorcan's uncompromising examination. Not that he'd been dressed that often in the last few weeks.

He caught himself drifting into a doze, so decided to get dried off. He lay on his bed wearing a pair of light pajama bottoms because it didn't feel right to call his aunt when he was naked. She answered the phone at the first ring. Rowan pulled Bilbo close but the expected tirade didn't come.

"Rowan love, it's wonderful to hear from you. How are you doing?"

"You know, I'd prefer if you just yelled at me. I'm sorry I haven't been able to call more often." Rowan rolled his eyes at Bilbo.

"And there was me trying for sweet and understanding." Rory snickered. "Should have known I couldn't pull that off. Now, what's up? There must be something or you wouldn't be calling me."

"You have a suspicious mind."

"And you're not denying it so spill."

Rowan debated how much to tell her but decided that she'd get the story out of him eventually anyway, so he might as well be honest from the start.

"I've been offered a new job. It's with the guest here at The Retreat, as his personal assistant."

There was a moment of silence.

"And you want to take it." It was a statement, not a question.

"I think so." Rowan stuck the phone beneath his chin so he could massage his temples. There was headache developing in a tight band around his head. "I like him, Rory. A lot."

"I'm guessing the job description involves a little more than keeping his diary and answering his calls."

"Yeah, but those are details I'm not going to share with you, so don't even ask."

"Spoilsport. You're all grown up, Rowan. You don't need me to help you make a decision like this."

"I think I've already made it, if I'm honest, but it helps to talk things through with someone who understands me. Everyone here is very kind and I've made some great friends, but I think this new opportunity will be even better for me."

"Then you should take it," Rory said. "But I want to meet him and that's not negotiable."

Rowan giggled. He could just imagine the kind of interrogation his aunt would subject Lorcan to. That would be fun to watch.

"Okay, I'm going to call Ed now while he's still between shifts. I'll let you know where I'll be once I know."

"You told me the client was American. You won't be moving abroad, will you?"

"I've been helping him house hunt over here. He'll probably have to rent somewhere for a while but he's looking for a place in London and another in the Cotswolds, so we won't be far away. His home is in San Francisco, so I imagine he'll want to spend some time there too."

"I'm hiding your passport until I've had the chance to make sure he's good enough for you."

Rowan didn't know what to say to that so he made his goodbyes and selected Ed's number from his contact list instead.

"Hey, kink boy. I thought someone locked you in a dungeon and threw away the key."

"Funny, Ed. You and Rory should get together. You'd make a good comedy duo."

"She'd have to be the straight guy."

Rowan groaned.

"So how's the rich, Dommy dude?"

"Dude?"

"He's from the U.S., isn't he?"

"The rich Dommy dude is in London."

"Oh, I get it. I only get a call when his highness is elsewhere. Charming."

"Sometimes I think I'd get more intelligent conversation out of Bilbo."

Ed snorted. "Has he met your bear yet? Hairy, cuddly, in competition for his affection?"

"Bears are more your type, Ed. And leave Bilbo out of this. I need advice. Dommy dude has offered me a job — and I can't believe I'm calling him that. He'd whip my arse if he found out."

"And you'd enjoy it. Wait…he did what?"

"Asked me to leave The Retreat and be his personal assistant…amongst other things." Rowan was glad Ed couldn't see his smile.

"You've gone all gooey."

"Have not!"

"Have. So, you're going to take it?"

"I… Yes, I think so."

"You don't *know* so? There are far too many rhymes in this conversation, by the way."

"It's a huge decision. Whatever I do, I'll be letting someone down and I hate that."

"Sometimes you have to put yourself first, Row. I know that's against your religion, but for once be selfish. What do *you* want?"

"I want *him*." Saying it made it real.

"There you go, then. Simple."

"Is it though? It's a job, not a relationship."

"Have you asked him that?" Ed snickered. "Of course you haven't. I think you need to talk to him. If he's as good a Dom as you say, he'll want to know what's worrying you, won't he?"

"'Spose," Rowan mumbled, knowing Ed was right.

"Uh-huh. Listen to Uncle Ed, for he is wise and all-knowing. I want to meet this bloke that has you all tied up in knots. He needs my seal of approval."

"You sound like Rory." Rowan pummeled a pillow, releasing some pent-up frustration.

"She and I have a date tomorrow for fish and chips." Ed smacked his lips together.

"Are you replacing me with my aunt?" Rowan whined.

"No, just making sure our mutual interests are discussed. That's you, by the way."

"Oh my God. I'm going. I'm psychologically scarred by the idea of my best friend and my aunt discussing my love life. I hope you're happy."

"Ecstatic. Ring me tomorrow with an update, 'kay?"

"If I can. Bye, Ed."

Rowan pulled the covers up and snuggled beneath them, hugging Bilbo close. The events of the day had caught up with him and he drifted into a doze, though sleep proved to be impossible. There were far too many thoughts and worries whirling around in his head and it was still several hours until Lorcan's return. He tried counting sheep but his mind managed to turn them into fanged, woolly mutants with glowing red eyes. Squeezing his eyes tight shut didn't help either and his nagging headache wouldn't go away. He tossed and turned, unable to get comfortable. Utterly miserable, he wished the time would pass quicker. He needed to confess his knowledge about Lorcan's past and make a final decision about his own future. Until then, peace of mind would remain out of reach.

* * * *

Lorcan got back into The Retreat just after midnight. He was surprised to find Luke waiting for him in the hall.

"I hope you had a good evening," Luke said. "I wanted to be here to reassure you that Rowan is okay. He had dinner with me and the kitchen staff. He was a little subdued and I suspect suffering from a headache, but he ate well and chatted with everyone. He went up to the Blue Room after the meal."

"I'm glad to hear it. I have to admit I spent most of my evening thinking about him and my friends noticed how distracted I was, hence the relatively early return. I just wanted to get back to him. I should be here taking care of him."

Luke nodded. "I understand. There's something else you should know. Rowan spent some time on the computer this afternoon — he was researching."

Lorcan didn't need Luke to tell him what Rowan had been curious about. "My past."

Luke nodded.

"I should have been open with him from the start. He experienced the long-term effects of what happened to me firsthand. I can understand him being curious about what must've happened to give me nightmares." He sighed. "I didn't forbid him to use the computer. I just wish I'd had the courage to tell him before he found out for himself. The full details aren't in the news reports. He must be wondering exactly what happened."

"I'd suggest it's time for the two of you to have an open conversation. I suspect he's conflicted about the job you've offered him because he doesn't want to let Mr. Hoffman down. I think I have a solution for that. I spoke to Carey earlier this evening and suggested that Rowan remains an employee of The Retreat."

"But..."

"Hear me out," Luke said. "He will remain an employee under contract, but be attached to you in the same capacity he has been here. That will give him security and take away the personal element of the agreement. He wants a relationship, not just a job. He needs to submit to you and this solution will remove some conflict of interest. The two of you will have the time you need to get to know each other better but it will remove the pressure he's feeling to make a decision too quickly."

Lorcan thought for a few minutes, pacing the hall, running the idea through his head.

"It's perfect. The ideal solution. I've never been in love so I'm not sure what I'm feeling. It must be the same for him. Here at The Retreat, reality is suspended and it's hard to think long-term." He extended a hand, which Luke shook. "Thank you, Luke. I can't tell you how much I appreciate your thoughtfulness." He thought he detected a hint of color on Luke's cheeks, but the light wasn't bright enough to be sure.

"Go to him. I doubt he's asleep."

Lorcan jogged up the stairs. He paused outside the door to the Blue Room, taking a couple of deep breaths before going inside. A single lamp provided light, the dim glow casting a shadow across one side of Rowan's face. A glint of blue gave his wakefulness away.

As soon as Lorcan pushed the door closed, Rowan slipped from the bed to his knees. The metal cage around his cock caught Lorcan's eye. Tracking his gaze, Rowan's hand strayed to his groin.

"You never left me, Sir."

"Come here, Rowan." Once Rowan was on his feet, Lorcan pulled him close. He cupped his neck with one hand, his ass with the other, then kissed him — gently at first then with increasing aggression. He was hard and the need to possess Rowan's body almost overwhelmed him.

"Get back into bed."

While Rowan slipped beneath the covers, Lorcan stripped. He joined Rowan in bed, so close that skin touched skin from hip to shoulder. He entwined their fingers.

"You want to know what happened to me?"

Rowan stiffened. "You know?"

"Did you think I wouldn't find out?"

"Please don't be mad." Rowan spoke in a whisper.

"I'm not angry, not with you. With myself — definitely. I should have been honest from the start about the cause of the nightmares."

Rowan moved to rest his head on Lorcan's shoulder. Lorcan nuzzled his hair, breathing in his scent.

"When you asked me how I knew I was a Dominant, I told you the truth. What I didn't explain was how much inner turmoil I went through to accept it. Can you imagine how it felt to want to do things to another man that had been done to me by force? How the hell could I ever expect to tie a man up, make him helpless, beat him, hold him down and fuck him…?" His voice trailed off. He'd told Rowan more than he'd told anyone since signing his statement for the police.

"It's not the same thing. Not even in the same universe." Rowan's breath hitched. "Consent. Everything you do to me, you do because I allow it. Want it. Need it."

"I know…but it took me a long time and a lot of therapy to understand and I still…still can't get those bastards out of my head."

"I'll help you, Sir."

"You already have. More than you know."

"I want to come with you when you leave, Sir." Rowan rolled over, straddling Lorcan's body. He knelt, making eye contact. Lorcan could detect no doubt in his eyes. He rose, positioning himself over Lorcan's erection.

"Wait. We need lube." Lorcan gripped Rowan's hips.

"I made sure I was ready for you, Sir."

For once, Lorcan allowed Rowan to take control. The warmth and grip of his channel was like coming home.

"Take the key from around my neck," Lorcan said. "You can remove the cage." He kept as still as he could while Rowan fiddled with the lock. As soon as he was free, his cock stiffened.

"Need to come so bad, Sir." Rowan began to rise and fall, fucking himself. He reached for his dick but Lorcan knocked his hand away.

"That's mine." One brief tug was all it took for Rowan to come all over Lorcan's hand and belly. He wailed, tears rolling down his cheeks, eyes squeezed shut. Watching his reaction was enough to push Lorcan toward his own orgasm. He thrust into Rowan's body, claiming him with his release. Then, for a while, the only sound was a combination of gasping breaths.

Lorcan pulled Rowan onto his chest, sealing them together. Exhaustion and relief combined to push him into sleep moments after Rowan's gentle snores vibrated through his body.

Epilogue

Rowan sat up in bed, propped against a pile of pillows, Lorcan's computer open in his lap. Lorcan emerged from the bathroom, toweling his hair and sending a spray of droplets everywhere. Rowan treated himself to a blatant examination of his Dom's naked form. He licked his lips. Lorcan's lean muscles and well-defined abs were an inspiration and, if it hadn't been for the fact that Lorcan had already taken him twice that morning, he would definitely have been hard. As it was, Rowan's dick barely managed to twitch. He shifted, grateful for the well-sprung mattress cushioning his behind. Lorcan had been particularly enthusiastic about delivering his morning discipline. It had been a treat to stay in bed while Lorcan went to the gym, though he had made a trip to the bathroom. After scrubbing his sticky skin, he'd changed the bed and luxuriated in the scent of clean sheets until Lorcan returned.

"Are you looking at those property details again?"

"Yes, Sir. I can't believe they accepted your offer so quickly."

"It will still be a few weeks before we can move in, but we will make another visit soon to measure up and start ordering some furniture. The cellar will make the most amazing dungeon."

"Considering how much time we spent in the one here over the last few days, you should have plenty of ideas."

"It was inspiring." Lorcan stretched out on the bed, hands behind his head. "I can't believe my four weeks here ends today. The Retreat has come to feel like home."

"The time's gone so fast. I'm a little scared about re-joining the real world, Sir." Rowan closed the computer and put it to one side. He snuggled close to Lorcan and was rewarded with a kiss and hug.

"You have absolutely nothing to be afraid of because you will be with me." Lorcan grinned. "And I won't be letting you out of my sight."

"Mr. Hoffman's flat is really close to The Underground. We are so lucky that one of his properties became available just at the time we needed it."

"Fate. Just like you and me. It was meant to be."

Lorcan patted his arse, making Rowan giggle.

"And we'll definitely be paying regular visits to the club. It's about time I got my money's worth out of my membership."

"I met some other subs when I was there for my interview. It will be good to have friends to talk to."

"You can always talk to me... Or Bilbo." Lorcan chuckled.

"Don't tease me, Sir. You weren't meant to find out about him."

"I'll let you into a secret. I have a partly chewed plush bunny back in San Francisco."

"You do?"

"I do. So I'm in no position to make fun of you. And I think it will be great if you have friends at the club, so long as they don't lead you astray."

Rowan pictured Olly in his head. "I'll be good, Sir. I promise."

"I almost hope you won't be. Punishments are fun."

"For you, Sir." Rowan rolled his eyes then gasped as Lorcan gripped his dick with a warm hand, stroking him to hardness. When Lorcan let go and slipped out of bed, Rowan pouted, but he didn't have to wait long for Lorcan to return carrying three strips of worn leather.

"I've had this collar and cuffs for a long time. They are worn because I used to put them on myself. For years after what happened, I had to train myself to tolerate the touch of leather on my skin. They used their belts, you see. I couldn't let them win, so at home, in private I wore these all the time hoping that one day I'd be able to put them on someone else."

He buckled the supple leather cuffs around Rowan's wrists before slipping the collar around his neck and once it was fastened, his attention returned to Rowan's rigid shaft.

"It's an honor that you wear them for me."

Rowan had no words. His eyes filled with tears. He pushed into Lorcan's fist, desperate for friction. When he came, the dam of his emotions broke and he sobbed, overcome by the joy of the moment.

"It's my honor to serve you, Sir."

"And mine to be served. You gave me back the future, Rowan. And I can't wait for us to explore it together." Lorcan nudged his knees apart. "And before we have to face our farewell breakfast, I feel the need to explore your body a bit more."

"I don't think there's a single inch left for you to discover, Sir."

"Best to be sure, though." Lorcan thrust inside him in one smooth movement, claiming him. Coherent thought was no longer a possibility. Rowan focused on his body, on sensation, and let his Master take control.

Want to see more from this author? Here's a taster for you to enjoy!

Owned by the Sea

L.M. Somerton

Excerpt

Jonty stood on the swaying deck and took a last, longing glance at the shore. His stomach was already heaving and the *Caroline*, named after his mother, had only just left the shelter of the bay. The next three days at sea were going to be torment. He hated the annual family ritual that took him away from his painting, but his father insisted on it and, at twenty-five, Jonty still hadn't found the courage to refuse him. Rex Trelawn, who headed a private bank when he wasn't torturing his son, had given up on Jonty ever being a 'proper' sailor, so Jonty was consigned to the galley with orders to keep the rest of the family fed and watered. He dealt with supplies, stocked the cupboards and made sure the boat was ready for a short sea voyage. He was also responsible for reporting their position to the coastguard at regular intervals, which he managed between visits to the head where his stomach contents insisted on making unwelcome reappearances.

The *Caroline* was a forty-six footer and manageable with a crew of four. She was just big enough that Jonty could avoid his father for some, if not all, of the trip. Rex always took the wheel while Jonty's mother and younger sister, Evie, managed ropes and sails with ease. Evie had a sturdy build and relished the challenges of sailing while Jonty favored his recently deceased grandfather, being slight and less than average height. They were a small family, just the four of them, and Jonty found it impossible to refuse the one outing of the year that brought them all together, much as he wanted to. Three days battling his father's disappointment was not his idea of a fun time.

Jonty slipped below deck to the narrow, claustrophobic galley and began preparations for a light supper. Soup and bread, fruitcake and hot chocolate would suffice — not that he'd be able to eat any of it himself. Just the idea of food made his stomach flip over. The four of them would take breaks and sleep in shifts, sailing out past Land's End and into the Atlantic during the night. It would be something of an endurance test but Jonty could cope with that. He kept strange hours when he painted, sometimes forgetting to sleep.

His father was first to descend into the cabin, brushing a hand through his windswept silver hair. He shed his waterproofs, hanging them on a peg before taking a seat at the table.

"Wind's getting up, Jonathon. Be sure to check the shipping forecast later."

"Yes, sir." Jonty didn't need the reminder, but said nothing. He ladled soup into a bowl then placed it in front of his father.

"Not eating?" The usual note of disapproval colored Rex Trelawn's tone.

"No." Jonty didn't expand. His father knew full well that Jonty got seasick every time he sailed.

"Come and join me."

Jonty held back a sigh. He wasn't feeling up to defending himself yet again.

"Shaw tells me your earnings are exceptional for such a young artist. He wants more work from you."

The sigh escaped. "Shaw has no business discussing my finances with you. He's my agent, not yours."

"I hope you're investing well?" Rex waved a soup spoon at him, ignoring Jonty's objection. "I'll have to put the rent up on Cliff House."

Jonty's family, including his sister who was studying at King's College, resided in London. Jonty chose to live at the family's second home in Cornwall where the pure light was perfect for painting. He needed a place of his own where he could cut another tie to his domineering father but somehow he'd never gotten around to house hunting. He didn't rise to Rex's taunt. Housing discussions were preferable to those that questioned his 'dubious lifestyle choices'. Rex Trelawn had never quite accepted his son's sexual orientation and it was a topic best avoided. When Jonty came out at eighteen, Evie had shrugged, his mother had wept for a while then refreshed her makeup, hugged him then commenced trawling her copious address book for prospective boyfriends. Rex had given him the silent treatment for months until Jonty's first gallery showing had sold out. He'd proved to have some worth, so they'd reached a truce of sorts.

"It's time I found a place of my own," he said. "Property is a good investment these days, isn't it?"

Rex grunted. Checkmate had been reached. Rex wanted his son as a live-in caretaker for Cliff House, a place where he had a hold on him. Rex knew it and so did Jonty. "It's time for the shipping forecast."

Jonty switched on the radio then relaxed into the familiar litany of strange names and wind speeds, paying particular attention to Lundy and Sole.

"It's brisker than I expected," Rex muttered. "Bloody weather changes on the toss of a coin. We could be in for a bumpy ride." He cut himself a slice of fruitcake, grinning.

Jonty's stomach did a jig. He just made it to the head in time.

An unpleasant five minutes later, Jonty returned to the cabin to find Evie swapping places with their father at the table.

"Have you been worshiping the porcelain god again, big brother?"

"The boy has a weak constitution," Rex grumbled, disappearing up the steps to the deck.

"And he could eat roadkill on a rollercoaster without retching," Jonty sniped. "You want soup, sis?"

"Only if you haven't thrown up in it." Despite her words, Evie's smile was sympathetic.

"There's nothing left in my stomach. Besides, you're like Dad. You'll eat anything." Jonty did his duty with the soup then watched as Evie demolished the entire bowl and two sizeable chunks of bread.

"Hungry work out there." She grinned. "Dad been giving you grief again?"

"Same as usual." Jonty shrugged. "He won't change."

"Next year when he proposes this trip, tell him to go take a running jump off the nearest pier."

"So says the favored child."

"I'm straight, gorgeous, I love sport and will provide him with grandchildren. You are not straight, far too pretty for a man, refuse to cut your hair, you hate sport and you have a talent he doesn't, which will no doubt make you richer than him. Of course he loves me best." She raised her mug of hot chocolate in a toast.

Jonty couldn't help but laugh. "Love you, sis."

"You too. Now get back to work, galley slave. Mum will be down here next expecting five-star service."

"Okay. You be careful up there. The forecast isn't great."

"Nice and bouncy. Just the way I like it."

Jonty groaned. Sometimes he wondered if he and Evie were actually related or if he'd been swapped at birth. He got a fifteen-minute respite before his mother showed up, dripping wet.

"It's getting a bit brisk out there." She shook out her wet outerwear. "I'm starving."

A violent swell threw Jonty from one side of the galley to the other. He banged his hip but managed to save the pan of soup, slamming the lid on. "In your language, 'a bit brisk' translates as blowing a gale. I hope no one wants hot food later. If this keeps up I won't be able to use the stove."

"You're looking a bit green, sweetheart." His mother took the spot Evie had vacated. She chugged down the soup, dunking bread to mop up every drop. "Mmm, fruitcake too, you're spoiling us! Have you eaten?"

"What do you think?" Jonty put a flask of hot chocolate on the table then wedged himself onto the bench.

"Found a nice boy yet?"

Jonty felt giddy. His mother switched from one topic to another more often than she changed her designer shoes. "I'm too busy and, besides, Cornwall is hardly a hotspot on the gay scene."

"Come up to London, then. There's this club I've heard about called The Underground…and another place called Secrets…"

"Mother! Those are BDSM clubs. Your internet history must be fascinating."

"I just thought… The Underground is in a very nice area. Westminster. Probably full of kinky MPs."

"We are not having this conversation. No. Just no." Jonty hid his face in his hands.

"Interesting that you already know what kind of clubs they are." His mother gave him a sly grin.

"I… Eat your fruitcake."

"If you weren't so green, I'm sure you'd be bright red. I'm your mother, not a nun. You and your sister are evidence that I have had sex at some point."

"I think I'm going to be sick again." Jonty ran for the shelter of the head where he slammed the door, grateful for the escape. "My own mother thinks I need to join the leather scene. Oh God, could this nightmare get any worse?" It wasn't that he'd discounted a possible visit to The Underground, which did appeal to him. It just wasn't a topic he wanted to discuss with his mother of all people. The boat lurched to one side then the floor seemed to drop from beneath his feet. Jonty staggered, trying to get his balance in the confined space. A need for air overwhelmed him. He burst back into the cabin to find himself alone.

The swell had increased so Jonty spent a few frantic minutes stowing everything that wasn't nailed down, gaining more than a few bruises in the process. He used the intercom to get an accurate map reference for their position from his father before reporting into the coastguard who warned him of increasingly heavy seas.

"No shit." Jonty grabbed the edge of the table to steady himself. He relayed the information to his father. "Do you think we should turn back?"

"No, of course not. We can ride it out. It's just a squall."

"I think it's a bit more than that," Jonty argued.

"Get some sleep, Jonathon. I'll wake you in six hours. It will all be over then and we'll be wishing for more wind, not less."

"I... Yes, sir." At sea, the captain's word was law and there was no room for dissension. Although with his father that applied at all times, not only onboard the *Caroline*, so Jonty knew he was fighting a losing battle. He did a quick tidy round then rolled into his bunk in the miniscule sleeping cabin, staying fully clothed. He drifted into an uncomfortable doze, rocking from side to side with the motion of the waves, his dreams filled with shipwrecks and towering seas.

* * * *

For Jonty, the next twenty-four hours were a nightmare of nausea and conditions straight out of hell. He'd had little sleep when his sister woke him because he was needed on deck. His father still insisted on pushing ahead with the journey even though the waves were topping twenty feet and growing. Even with his safety line firmly attached, Jonty felt vulnerable, but his mother needed rest so he ignored his roiling stomach and followed his sister's orders. When the wind dropped and he finally got a break he was soaked through, despite his waterproofs, and freezing. His hands and face were raw from salt and wind burn.

"Looks like we made it through!" His father sounded triumphant despite having been at the wheel all night.

"I'm going to catch forty winks while Evie takes the wheel." He stomped below, not even glancing in Jonty's direction.

"I don't think this is over," Jonty said, watching the wind whip foam from the tips of the waves. The huge swell had subsided and a glimpse of gold peeked between threatening clouds. "We're in the eye of the storm."

"This isn't a hurricane, Jonty." Evie laughed. "Admit it—Dad was right. We rode it out. As soon as Mum gets back on deck, you can go below and cook. I could use something hot."

Jonty shrugged. He wasn't an expert sailor and his empty guts were hardly a good indicator of conditions, but it seemed to him that the weather had changed too quickly. Conditions at sea were often unpredictable, but he was eager to get back on the radio and check the forecast. If his suspicions were unfounded then great, he'd hold up his hands and bow to his father's superior instincts. "I hope you and Dad are right."

"The wind's good. Help me get the mainsail up, Jonty." His mother appeared next to him.

"How come you look so refreshed?" he asked. "I feel like I slept for about five minutes and that was on a possessed trampoline."

"After years of your father's sailing expeditions, I've learned to sleep anywhere." She smiled. "It was good of you to come along, Jonty. I know you'd rather be anywhere else."

Jonty helped with the sails then headed below. He had stashed pre-cooked chili that just needed heating through. His stomach rebelled at the thought of eating anything, but the others would appreciate the hot food. Once the meal was underway, he checked the forecast. The satellite images made for uncomfortable viewing.

From what he could tell, the *Caroline* had passed through the edge of one storm and was currently riding a gap between two more. The boat was being funneled toward a potential convergence. It was still possible that the storm centers might dissipate and Jonty prayed that would happen. He got on the long-range radio to contact the coastguard.

"This is the *Caroline*. Repeat, this is the *Caroline*. Any update on prevailing conditions?"

"*Caroline*. Glad to hear from you. We were starting to worry."

"It was a bit hairy for a while but we're through without damage."

"You didn't turn back?"

"No... Please hold while I get current coordinates." Jonty radioed his sister to check their position, then reported back.

"Not good, *Caroline*. You're headed into a real mess out there."

"I see it." Jonty sighed. "Any sign of separation?"

"Met. Office says convergence is most likely. Can you outrun it?"

"Negative." Jonty took a deep breath. "What's your advice?"

"Batten down the hatches and pray, *Caroline*. Keep us updated and Godspeed."

"*Caroline* out." Jonty sighed. He had to wake his father and tell him the bad news. He ventured into the cabin and for a while stood watching his father sleep. Rex looked younger, less severe, in repose. Taking a deep breath, Jonty shook his father awake.

"What...what is it, Jonathon?" Rex scrubbed a hand through his hair.

"Storms are converging. We're running into trouble with no way out. The coastguard expected us to turn around. They have no advice other than to hunker down."

"You're exaggerating."

"Come and see for yourself." Jonty's patience was running thin.

Rex hauled himself out of his bunk. He pulled on a sweater but had otherwise remained dressed while he slept. "Fine. This better not be a false alarm." As Rex stepped through the cabin door, the boat lurched violently to one side. He lost his balance and pitched forward. Jonty, following behind, tried to catch him but missed and fell himself. There was a sickening crack from his arm as he landed, then a moment of blinding pain.

"Shit. Fuck!" He knew the arm was broken. There were no bones sticking out but his wrist was already swelling. He cradled it, taking deep breaths while the pain subsided to a throb. "Dad, are you okay?" Jonty scrambled to his feet as the boat pitched and rolled, the brief respite in the weather clearly over. He made it into the main cabin and found his father face down on the floor. Blood formed a pool around his head.

"Oh God, no." Jonty dropped to his knees. He tried to see where the blood was coming from. His father was out cold, his head at a strange angle. Jonty swallowed his fear. He leaned down, trying to detect any breath from his father's mouth. He felt nothing, nor could he find a pulse. "You can't do this now, you fucker." Jonty's anger overwhelmed him. A life-or-death situation approached and his father, who'd gotten them into this position, had taken the easy way out. Even with his limited first aid training, Jonty understood he shouldn't move his father in case of a back or neck injury, but he had to balance that with a need to get him breathing. He rolled him over, pushing back his panic as he noted the blood leaking from Rex's left ear. He made sure his father's airway was clear then began mouth to mouth. After what seemed like hours but was no more than a minute, his father gave a small moan. He didn't regain consciousness and his breath was shallow, but he was alive. He was a big man and there was no way Jonty could move him on his own. He shoved a cushion under his head then covered him with an unzipped sleeping bag from the cabin. With Rex as comfortable as Jonty could make him, Jonty got on the radio to his sister.

"Evie, check the satellite—we have big problems and Dad's had a fall down here. He's unconscious." He didn't mention that Rex had stopped breathing for a while, nor that he suspected his injuries to be severe.

"Is he…?"

"He's in a bad way, Evie. Head injury and I've broken my arm."

"I can't leave the wheel, Jonty. Let me tell Mum what's going on. You'd better get kitted up. We're going to need you up here, even with one arm out of action."

Jonty strapped his wrist into a temporary splint from the first aid kit then swallowed some painkillers. He did a cursory clean-up of the chili pan, which had crashed to the floor, splattering the spicy meat everywhere. It was a few minutes he didn't have but he didn't want to leave a hazard for someone else to slip on. He struggled into his still-wet gear, shuddering at the cold before making his way onto the deck and into hell. It was hard to tell whether it was day or night. The angry purple and black clouds merged with the sea. The noise assaulted Jonty's ears, with the howl of the wind challenging the roar of towering surf like two predators fighting for dominance. Jonty got his safety line attached then worked his way forward. He could just make out his mother through the spray. When he reached her, she grabbed his shoulder, holding him close.

"We need to show as little sail as possible. Get the main down and the storm jib up. Once we've done that we'll assess our position." She had to scream to make herself heard. She didn't ask about Rex, but Jonty could see the fear in her eyes. "Your arm. Can you do it?"

He nodded—it wasn't as if he had a choice—then set to work. The stinging spray blinded him and only his gloves prevented the skin from being flayed from his hands. At one point the ship rolled almost ninety degrees before righting itself. Jonty fell, slithering across the deck before he managed to grab hold of a stanchion and get some purchase. The pain made him sick and he retched. He hauled himself up then lurched toward his mother. "This is crazy. We're fighting a losing battle. We need to send a mayday."

An ear-splitting crack sounded above his head. He glanced up then dived for cover as the mast toppled like a felled pine, bringing the rigging with it. Jonty hit the deck, covering his head with his arms. He sprawled, rolling with the movement of the waves, expecting to be crushed at any moment, but the blow never came. He tried to rise but ropes were tangled around his ankles. Between them and the rolling pitch of the boat it took an age to struggle to his feet.

"Mum!" Frantic, Jonty peered through the spray. A huge wave crashed over the side of the boat, knocking him down again, soaking him, filling his mouth with saltwater. He retched as he struggled to his knees. He gave up attempting to stand and crawled toward the downed mast. His hand made contact with a rubber boot, then a leg. Scrubbing the water from his eyes,

Jonty struggled to comprehend what he was seeing. His mother's legs stuck from beneath the mast, which had fallen across her chest. When he climbed over it, he could see she was gone, crushed beneath its weight, her sightless eyes open and staring at the sky. A sluggish stream of blood, diluted by the rain and spray, trickled from her mouth. Jonty screamed his anguish into the wind, the sound torn away in an instant. Intense cold and pain permeated every atom of his being. "Evie." *I have to get to Evie.*

Evie had lashed herself to the wheel but it had been ripped from her hands.

"The steering's gone, Jonty. The rudder must have sheared off. Where's Mum?"

"She's gone." Jonty sobbed his response. "She's dead, Evie. The mast…"

Evie froze, her mouth open in a soundless scream. Jonty pushed aside his own emotions. "Get below. There's nothing you can do up here. I'll send up a flare. You try the radio. The waves are too high to launch the life raft. Our best chance is to stay with the boat." He untied the rope around Evie's waist. "Keep the safety line on until you're through the cabin door." She nodded, though Jonty suspected it was an automatic response. He ripped off his gloves then groped in the locker beneath the wheel for the flare gun. Working with one good but frozen hand meant getting it loaded took an age and, when he finally fired the arc of light into the sky, Jonty had little hope it would be seen. The flare lit the deck and, to Jonty's horror, he saw Evie attempting to reach their mother.

"Evie! No!" Jonty scrambled after her, half crawling as the deck dropped from beneath his feet. He grabbed her. "There's nothing you can do. Get below!"

"We can't leave her out here, Jonty."

"We can't shift the mast, Evie. What are you hoping to achieve apart from killing yourself?" Jonty knew his words were hard but they were necessary. He hauled his sister back toward the cabin door then half shoved her through, releasing her lifeline at the last minute. She staggered down the steps where she collapsed in a heap on the floor. Jonty fought the door until it closed before falling next to her. He groaned as his broken arm was jarred.

"See how Dad is, Evie," Jonty snapped. He dragged himself to the radio. "Mayday, mayday, this is the *Caroline*. Our mast is down and rudder gone. We have casualties needing urgent assistance. Mayday. Mayday." The handset was ripped from his grasp as the boat tilted and this time kept going. Pots, pans and crockery became a barrage of missiles as the boat turned turtle and, for a few seconds, Jonty found himself on the ceiling of the cabin. The boat righted itself and Jonty slithered down a wall, crashed into a cupboard and finally came to rest beneath the table. Water sloshed around him, the level above his knees. A warm trickle ran down his cheek and he brushed at the sensation, his hand coming away stained with blood.

"Jonty?" Evie crawled toward him, her skin bone-white. "I think I broke a rib."

"I'm here." He wedged himself into a corner then pulled Evie against him, being as gentle as he could, putting her back to his chest.

"Dad's… He's…gone."

"Hush." He smoothed his sister's dripping hair, not wanting to accept the implications of her words. "It's going to be okay."

"I don't want to die, Jonty."

"We'll be fine. I'm sure help is on its way," Jonty lied. He was so tired. His vision blurred and tears rolled down his cheeks as grief swamped him. Evie stilled in his arms and he couldn't decide whether it was a good or bad thing. She was exhausted, probably hypothermic and in shock, but he couldn't wake her. Her breath came in slow rasps. He had never felt so alone. He closed his eyes and let the darkness take him.

About the Author

Lucinda lives in a small village in the English countryside, surrounded by rolling hills, cows and sheep. She started writing to fill time between jobs and is now firmly and unashamedly addicted.

She loves the English weather, especially the rain, and adores a thunderstorm. She loves good food, warm company and a crackling fire. She's fascinated by the psychology of relationships, especially between men, and her stories contain some subtle (and some not so subtle) leanings towards BDSM.

L.M. loves to hear from readers. You can find her contact information, website details and author profile page at http://www.pride-publishing.com.